MW01488984

Beyond Betwixt Between

Carla J. Nelson

Illustrations by
Christina R. Harshman

Botanical Renderings
Dover Publications, New York, NY

Herb Gatherings, Incorporated
Lafayette, Indiana

Beyond Betwixt Between

Library of Congress Catalog Number:
98-92970

ISBN 0-9664662-0-9

10 9 8 7 6 5 4 3 2 1

Published by:
Herb Gatherings, Incorporated
10949 E 200 S
Lafayette, IN 47905

Printed and bound in the United States of America

To Rich,
who transforms my dreams into realities.

To Christie and Kate,
who first welcomed Lyla into our midst.

&
To Austin Richard,
my own "darling dear", the
precious grandson who will
transcend my circle of life
and, hopefully, carry the torch of
understanding and attunement,
into a new generation. May the
nature spirits be with you always,
as you are with me.

Tell me a story,
Of tinkling fairy bells,
Of fairy rings and fairy dust,
Fairy stones and shells.

Tell me a story
Of shimmering fairy wings,
Of fairy herbs, flowers and trees,
And all those fairy things.

Carla J. Nelson

A portion of the proceeds from this book will fund the Herb Gatherings Grant Program. These grants provide seed money to qualifying individuals and groups for projects that involve planting threatened/endangered native species, or teaching children about herbs and native plants. Contact the publisher for details.

Chapter One

"Tell me a story, Grandma", Austin urged. "A fairy story, with a boy in it!"

"Well, let me see!" his grandmother said, taking a moment to mull this over before proceeding. "Once upon a time . . ."

"No, no!" Austin objected. "I don't want to hear a 'once upon a time fairy tale'. I want to hear a *now* fairy tale! There are fairies *now* aren't there?"

She hesitated. "Well, most people don't believe so, but I do. In fact, I'll tell you about a family of fairies that was recently Betwixt Between.

"Betwixt Between! What does that mean?"

His grandmother smiled at his pensive face and chuckled softly. "You know Austin, that's what Pitter wanted to know and that's where the trouble began. But I must start at the beginning."

Austin laid his head back and snuggled up closer to his grandmother on the cozy couch. Blue flames licked out through the orange and red ones in the fireplace grate creating a mesmerizing dance of color and motion. Eyes filled with wonder, he listened as the magic story unfolded.

Not very long ago and not so far away, deep in the forest in a place local folks called The Golden Valley, there lived a band of fairies. For many years they made their home in this special place, tending the trees and the streams and the plants that lived there. And this was where the twins, Pitter and Patter were born. Those might seem like strange names but not so strange when you learn they were born during a spring rainstorm. Their mother, Lyla, was so soothed by the raindrops going *pitter-patter* on the roof of her little home, that she decided to name her new babies for them.

Pitter and Patter were delightful little boys, but one thing was obvious from the very beginning. While Patter was quiet and obedient and always had nice things to say, his brother Pitter, was just the opposite. Since fairies do not like loud, obnoxious people, or anyone who brags or tells untrue stories or breaks the rules, Pitter was most always in trouble. He liked to pull pranks on everyone. He pried into everyone's business and sometimes even gossiped - both very objectionable activities to fairies.

And then there was the matter of *sleep-flying*. Fairies in Pitter's family always sleep during the day, then work and play all night. But not Pitter. He had an unusual problem. In the middle of the day, when everyone else was fast asleep, including himself, he would become aware that he was no longer in his cozy bed of milkweed down. Instead, he would be in a strange forest, surrounded by beautiful, fragrant plants. Whenever this happened, he would be filled with a wild mixture of emotions. Afraid and lonely one minute, and excited and curious the next. What was this place and why was he drawn to it over and over against his will? He never planned to sleep-fly. It just happened. And always he ended up in the same place, not knowing how he got there or how to find his way back. It was very upsetting. Each time, he would cry himself back to sleep and before long, he was once again in The Golden Valley, safe in his own little bed. He never knew how he got *there* either. Sometimes, he arrived back in late evening just as the other fairies were waking up. They were most disturbed by all of this and talked about it behind his back. They came to pity Lyla and Patter for having such an errant boy in their family. "How embarrassing," they chided. "How disappointing. Too bad Pitter can't be a good boy like his brother. Patter is so perfect! Truly a mother's joy - not a problem child like Pitter!"

The situation was further complicated by the fact that Pitter was the grandson of the Fairy King and in line to be their leader some day. How could this ever be? They feared he was too head-strong, too disrespectful, too irresponsible to ever sit on the throne. But he was the firstborn. Only *he* could be king. How could their clan survive with someone so unfit to lead them?

Lyla heard the whisperings - each one a dart pricking her tender heart. Pitter wasn't a bad boy. He was just - *different*. If only everyone could see the goodness in him instead of his unusual *almost-human* side. She worried about Pitter and what the future held for him. She blamed herself for forgetting to have the midwife hang a sprig of vervain over the doorway when the boys were born to ward off the Evil Ones. Had Pitter been cursed? The possibility hung over her like a dark, menacing cloud. She knew there was talk from time to time at the Fairy Council about banishing him. How could she ever live if they did? She loved both her boys the same and the thought of losing either of them filled her with fear and sadness.

One evening in early springtime, shortly after the sun had set below the distant hills, all the fairies were unexpectedly sum-moned to the Fairy Council. Everyone hurriedly tidied themselves and scurried off to the Meeting Ring deep in the dark woods. But Lyla lingered behind wringing her hands. Pitter was missing and she knew he must once again be off sleep-flying. His absence at the meeting would surely be noticed and bring more unwelcome atten-tion to his troubling behavior. She knew his grandfather was run-ning out of patience and any further episodes might well bring about an unpleasant punishment. Just as she was about to give up and hurry off to the gathering alone, a flicker of purple light caught her eye. At last, here was her darling dear! Pitter flew down through the treetops and landed beside Lyla, rubbing the sleep from his eyes. He looked disoriented and confused and Lyla's heart went out to him.

"Pitter," she scolded good naturedly. "What am I *ever* going to do with you?" We're late for a council meeting and you know Grandfather will not be pleased. We must hurry!"

Still a bit dazed from another troubling sleep-flying episode, Pitter quickly made himself presentable. Off they flew to the Deep Woods. They stopped just short of the Meeting Ring to take in the situation. As expected, everyone else was already in place. Pitter was always awed by the sight of the Meeting Ring which was only used on very rare, special occasions. A huge old fallen log covered with tier after tier of spongy brown fungi provided the seating. And every seat was filled, except for the two down front reserved for Lyla and Pitter. Beyond the fallen log was a large ring of soft, emerald green moss. In the center were two toadstool thrones. On one sat Pitter's grandfather - the King, and on the other sat his grandmother - the Queen. They were his father's parents. And while he loved them, he found them a bit stuffy and rigid.

He could see them frowning now. A look of piercing disapproval shown from the King's eyes as Lyla and Pitter quietly took their places next to Lyla's mother and Patter in the front row. Everyone shifted uncomfortably in their seats fearing this might be the day the King's anger finally got the best of him. And who could blame him? But the King had other things on his mind tonight that took precedence over his grandson's behavior problem. With an air of royal authority he called the meeting to order.

"We have come together to discuss the admittance of a new family into our midst. A group from beyond our boundaries have approached the outer guards and asked if they might join us and live among us. They seem to be a fine family of fairies, although a bit unkempt. This condition is most unfortunate but justified because of . . . , well . . .," the King cleared his throat nervously, then added, "unavoidable circumstances, which will be remedied

4

forthwith. Therefore, I recommend that we offer them our hospitality for as long as they like. What say ye?"

It was the custom for the King to always end his presentations with 'what say ye' when in fact, everyone knew it didn't matter what anyone else thought. It was understood that the King had already made the decision for them which was exactly what they wanted the King to do. As tradition dictated, they all rose as one, saluted the King with their wands and proclaimed in unison, "Your wish is ours, dear King."

Pleased, the King stood up and made a motion. Out of the shadows behind him, tiptoed a band of some twenty fairies - adults and children. When they reached the King, they bowed and curtsied and then turned toward the multitude of fairies watching attentively from the row of seating on the oak log. In a booming voice the King proclaimed, "I give you our new members. Welcome them and rejoice in their arrival."

With that the fairies left their places and rushed forward to greet the newcomers. Since fairies never pass up an opportunity to engage in partying, a fine celebration was soon underway. Musicians retrieved their instruments from storage places inside the hollow log and festive tunes soon filled the wooded glen. While couples twirled daintily on the velvet moss carpet, others stood around the outside watching, clapping with the music, and talking.

Pitter, relieved that his grandfather had not made an issue of his late arrival at the meeting, was once again in good spirits. His apprehension about being punished for his tardiness was quickly forgotten. In its place was a gnawing curiosity about the new members. He could see, even from a distance, that their clothes were soiled and their wings were dull and dingy. Why ever would fairies be so lax about their appearance? It was a fairy's duty to always be clean and spotless. And their wings must always shimmer. This group of fairies was certainly not measuring up. So why didn't

Grandfather find their appearance offensive, Pitter wondered. He *always* found Pitter's behavior offensive and never hid his displeasure. The more Pitter thought of this, the more resentful he became.

"Oh, Oh!" Patter exclaimed looking at Pitter suspiciously. "I don't like that look on your face, Pitter. You're worrying me. You're not plotting some sort of scheme, are you? You're already in so much trouble."

Pitter scowled at his twin brother and without a word flitted off toward the conclave of fairies surrounding the newcomers. Everyone was engaged in lively conversation but no one seemed to be asking the questions Pitter wanted answers to. He shifted from foot to foot impatiently, watching and listening. Finally, he saw a young fairy boy about his age, standing off to the side. He was one of *them.* It was obvious by his grimy appearance, Pitter thought with disgust. Unable to control his curiosity any longer, Pitter approached the boy.

"Hello", he said. "My name is Pitter."

"Hello, it's nice to meet you," the newcomer answered. "I'm Gil."

Then they both bowed sideways, lightly touching their wing tips on their right sides together. This was the polite way fairies introduced themselves to each other. Before long the two were talking like old friends. Pitter told Gil all about The Golden Valley, which fairy girls were the best dancers, and where the sweetest dew for sipping could be found. Soon Gil was very much at ease, which was exactly what Pitter had hoped for. Now, with a little skillful prying he could find out what he really wanted to know. Looking down at his own tunic Pitter coyly remarked, "Oh, my, it looks like I've gotten a little bit of dirt on me! I should probably hurry home and clean this off. You know how everyone is about cleanliness?"

Gil hung his head and muttered something about not seeing

6

any dirt on Pitter. Pitter could tell he was uncomfortable but instead of letting the subject drop, he forged on. "Come to think of it," he mused. "Your tunic could use a little washing too!"

"Don't you think I know that?" blurted Gil. "I don't look this way because I want to! I *want* to be clean. We all want to be clean. Why do you think we came here?" He was on a roll now and the words just spilled out, toppling over each other as he went on and on. "It's been terrible! First, the plant upstream from us dumped toxic waste in the water. You can't imagine the awful results. All the fish died, and so did the frogs and the tadpoles - all our water friends. It was just *awful*! Then the burning started! Just north of us they cut down acres and acres of trees for new development. They made huge piles of logs and limbs and shrubs and leaves and old tires and rubbish and set it all on fire. For days a thick heavy cloud of smelly smoke hung over our forest, covering everything in black soot. Many birds died. There were bird bodies everywhere. Just when we thought things couldn't get any worse, the plants started to die. The soapwort, the foxglove, the mayapples, the lady's slipper, the bloodroot, - all gone. There was nothing left to clean with and nothing left to eat. Some of our wee ones died. Finally, we had to admit the worst." Here Gil stopped, cleared his throat, and looked around sheepishly.

"The worst?" Pitter asked. He was having a hard time believing all of this and wondered if Gil wasn't making this all up.

"Well, yes! Gil insisted. "You know - the worst thing that can happen to a fairy clan!"

"No I don't know", Pitter shot back. "What are you talking about?"

"We were, - well, Betwixt Between!", he whispered.

Pitter looked at Gil for a moment, pondering those two words over and over in his head. He had a vague recollection of having heard them before but had no idea what they meant. He decided

Gil was just being dramatic or making a joke. Either way he wasn't falling for it. Betwixt Between, indeed!" Whoever heard of such a thing? Betwixt Between? What does that mean? Why that rhymes, Pitter thought and he was quite proud of himself for thinking of it. He loved rhymes. Instantly, he was kicking up his heels and dancing a jig around Gil, all the while chanting, "Betwixt Between. What does it mean? Betwixt Between. What does it mean?"

He was so caught up in his chanting and high-stepping that he failed to see the stir he was causing. All around him, the older fairies stood frozen in their places, staring at him in shock. Some covered their faces in disbelief. Some gasped and fainted on the ground. Others began to sob. The younger ones, frightened by all of this, flew off and hid in the bushes. Still Pitter danced on, his chant growing louder and louder, his arms waving and his feet kicking higher and higher. Then all at once, there was a brilliant flash of blinding light that startled even Pitter. He stopped abruptly in mid stride and looked around.

He couldn't believe his eyes. He was surrounded by anguished looks and disapproving stares. He blinked and looked again. What was the matter with everyone, he wondered. Then from behind him a loud voice bellowed. "That's it!! That's *it*!!! You have gone too far this time!" Pitter turned slowly to face the King. He had never heard that tone of voice from his grandfather before. He knew at once he was in very big trouble. He stood at attention and waited for his grandfather to continue. The King stood silently for a moment looking at Pitter with a mixture of anger and pity. He had so hoped this boy would grow up and shed his careless, almost human ways. Boyish pranks were one thing. His behavior this time, another. If there was to be any hope for his grandson, the King knew he could not go easy now. He loved his grandson, but Pitter was not fit to be King. And what were they to do if Pitter could not take his place. Only the firstborn could be King. He had to teach him a lesson - force him to grow up and mend his ways. He approached Pitter who was now greatly worried.

"What is wrong, Grandfather?" he asked. "What did I do to make everyone so upset?"

"My boy, how could you have reached the age you are and not have learned more about the vital matters? You are your father's son. My successor. How can you not know the gravity of what you just did?" With each question the King's voice rose higher and shriller, causing everyone to shrink back in fear.

Pitter looked at his feet and twisted his hands nervously behind his back but didn't answer.

"Let me see your silver pouch," the King ordered.

Pitter reached under his tunic and unfastened a small shiny bag from a gold cord around his waist and silently handed it to his grandfather. His grandfather opened it carefully and reached in. He pulled out a small brown object as big as his hand and held it out to Pitter.

"What is this?" he asked.

"A fairy stone", Pitter muttered.

"And where did it come from?"

"My father gave it to me."

"But where did it *come* from?"

"I don't know." Pitter answered.

"Didn't your father tell you when he gave this to you?"

"Well, maybe he did." he said trying to think back. Then vague memories stirred in his brain. He brightened. Then his face fell again. "I guess he started to. But I must have fallen asleep - or something! I just don't remember. Is it important?" At this all the older fairies who had gathered close to listen, swooned and gasped. Pitter was stricken by the looks on their faces. "Tell me, Grandfather", he pleaded finally. "Where did the stone come from and what does it have to do with all of this now?"

The King shook his head slowly in disbelief. To think he must explain this - - to Pitter of all fairies! "Listen and listen well," he said gruffly. "And all of you younger ones watching - you listen well too. This stone is a symbol of the saddest time in the history of our own fairy clan. It is a remembrance of a time when we too were Betwixt Between. Many, many years ago, long before my own grandfather's grandfather was born, our clan lived in a magnificent valley to the east not far from where the sun rises out of The Great Sea. There were no humans there then. The land was rich with dense forests and beautiful meadows. There were thousands of different woodland plant families and hundreds of wild animals of all shapes and sizes. The streams were as pure as glistening dewdrops and filled with many kinds of fishes, frogs and turtles. Our Ancient Ones lived in abundance and harmony. Then one day, a Traveler arrived in their midst. He was a fairy from a distant land. Washed out to sea in a violent storm, he was adrift for many moon cycles before finally reaching land. He wandered for a long time, looking for Wee Folk like himself. He was close to death when he stumbled into that enchanted kingdom. It took many days to nurse him back to health. It was then he told the story."

"Some years before, a Child King had been born in that far away land. A King that was both human and divine. He had no interest in riches and worldly things but promised untold happiness in the afterlife to all who followed him. The Ancient Ones rejoiced in this news and were very happy for the humans. They had no experience with humans but they had heard stories from other Travelers. They knew the humans were always searching for true happiness and never seemed able to find it. This King could be their answer. But the story the Traveler told that day had a tragic twist. When the Child King grew older, the humans turned on him. They humiliated him and beat him and hung him on a cross

10

to die. When the Ancient Ones heard this they were grief stricken beyond all words. One by one, they began to cry until great choking sobs filled the forest. And then a very strange thing happened. As each tear fell to the ground, it hardened into a brown shape, much like the cross the Traveler told about. This made everyone cry even more. Before long the ground was covered with hard brown crosses. Layer upon layer. Soon there was no place to stand without stepping on crosses. Everywhere, they were surrounded by the sad reminders of that terrible tragedy. So deep was their sadness that they could not work or sing or sleep. At last the King (my own great, great grandfather), had no choice but to call a Fairy Council and declare they were Betwixt Between."

As Grandfather uttered the words, Pitter heard a faint gasp ripple through the fairy throng standing watch. Solemnly, the King continued. "They wandered many miles and many moon cycles before finding this Golden Valley. You asked, 'Betwixt Between. What does it mean?' It signifies a time when through circumstances beyond our control we must leave our home, everything we know and love, forever - with no idea of where or when we will find another. It means quite simply, 'we can no longer stay here, but we have no place to go'. Those two words are the most dreaded words in all the kingdom. They are never to be spoken lightly. They are never to be ridiculed as you just did."

"I didn't know Grandfather," Pitter offered remorsefully.

"But you should have." the King retorted. "I *know* your father told you. You just didn't pay attention, as usual. This stone I hold in my hand, is a stone from our old home - the one the Ancient Ones had to abandon so many years ago. It is a fairy tear turned to stone - a forever remembrance of a time of grief and tragedy. It has been passed on from generation to generation. This one was your father's. It should be held in deepest reverence ."

"I'm sorry I didn't pay attention before, Grandfather," Pitter

11

stammered. "I don't understand how I could have forgotten something so important. I'll try to do better from now on."

The King stared at Pitter for a long time and then sighed a heavy sigh. "We've had this conversation before Pitter and nothing changes. I'm sorry too, but I must teach you a hard lesson." With that the King tapped Pitter's hand with his wand and a strange set of circles appeared. Beginning with a small blue circle in the center, then a larger green one, and an even larger orange one, and so on until there were eight circles with all the shades of a rainbow on the back of Pitter's left hand.

"The Circles of Attunement?!" Pitter asked incredulously.

"Yes!" Grandfather said emphatically. "If you are ever to be King, you must learn control and understanding. You must learn that the good of all must be placed before personal pleasure. The Circles mark you as one who is out of attunement. They will disappear one by one as you demonstrate your worthiness to be a responsible member of our kingdom."

Pitter stared at the circles on his hand. This was more than he had expected. With resentment and anger welling up inside him, he raised his eyes to his grandfather's and started to object. The stern, piercing look returned by the King, stopped him cold. Pitter turned slowly and scanned the faces of the other fairies encircling them. He could tell they all supported the King's action. He looked at his hand again and was overcome with rage. He glared at his grandfather, then without a word, snapped his fingers. Amid gasps of shock and a blinding flash of red and purple light, he disappeared.

The King sighed helplessly , then slowly made his way back to his throne. He sat down heavily. The Queen patted his hand and looked at him anxiously. She knew how much it hurt him to have to discipline Pitter so severely. But it was the only way, if Pitter was to ever be King. The other fairies collected themselves and went back to their evening chores and merrymaking. What was done, was done.

With a heavy heart, Lyla hurried home, hoping Pitter would be there. She accepted that his behavior needed a stern hand. But the Circles of Attunement were the last step before total banishment. Lyla could not bear to think of that. How could she ever go on if she lost her darling dear boy forever? When she arrived home, she found Pitter packing his treasure bag as Patter tried in vain to convince him to stay.

"What do you care?" Pitter demanded.

"You *know* I care. You're my brother." Patter shot back.

"Exactly!", Pitter countered sarcastically. "With me out of the picture, I'm sure Grandfather will find a way to bend the rules and make *you* the king. Tell me you don't *want* it. Tell me everyone else doesn't want it. I know you've always been everyone's favorite - even Momma's."

Overhearing this exchange sent a stab of pain clear to the core of Lyla's heart. "Stop it!" she cried. "That isn't true. I have always loved both of you equally. There are no favorites in my heart. Please, Pitter. Patter and I will help you with the Lessons of Attunement. The Circles will be gone in no time and everything will be as it should be. Just don't leave. I can't bear to lose you. *We* can't bear to lose you. Grandfather is growing old and frail. Only *you* can take his place. That's the Law of Faerie. You must be ready. You must stay."

Pitter was moved by the look of pain in his mother's eyes. "I'm sorry, Momma," Pitter whispered. "I just lose control. I don't understand why. Father would be so disappointed in me. I'm disappointed in myself. Everyone is." He fumbled with his bag, not knowing what to do. He felt so humiliated and genuinely sorry for all the trouble he had caused. At last he said, "If you and Patter and Grandmother can forgive me, I'll try to do better. I'll stay and try to make you proud."

"You know we forgive you, and you can be sure we will help you Pitter," Lyla promised.

Pitter thanked them both and hugged them. He felt a heavy sense of weariness creep through him. "If you don't mind, I am very tired," he said. "I'd just like to get a good day's sleep."

"The sun will be rising before long," Patter said. "Go on to bed. We'll talk more tonight."

Pitter hugged his mother and brother again, then retrieving his milkweed down pillow from his treasure bag, he flew up into the sprawling branches of a wild cherry tree and found a cozy nook. He positioned the pillow and laid his head on its welcoming softness. From below, the soothing strains of his mother's singing wafted up through the branches. The disgrace and turmoil of the night, made sleep hard to come by. He laid awake a long time thinking back over his life.

Thoughts of his father came flooding back. Too late, he remembered the tragic story of the fairy stone. His father *had* told him - the day he unexpectedly passed into the Other Realm. The memory of that terrible day, and the long, sad days that followed, opened up a well of grief Pitter had buried deep inside. While it was no excuse, he realized now that his bad behavior had been his futile attempt to cover up an aching heart.

The sun had risen bright above the horizon before Pitter finally fell into a restless sleep. A while later, while slumber ruled over the fairy kingdom of The Golden Valley, the outer guards saw a familiar purple light flash past overhead. Shaking their heads, they made a routine entry in the watch log. "Pitter observed sleep flying --- *again!*"

Chapter Two

Justin had not slept well all night. He missed his parents. He tried to understand how important their work was, but he hated it when it took them away from him. This time they would be gone for five months. The fact that they were halfway around the world in what newscasters called a 'trouble spot', made things even worse. His grandmother had stayed with him until school was over for the year. Then they had packed the car and made the long trip to Grandmother's house.

It wasn't that he didn't love it here. His friends at school would never believe this place. His grandmother called it her own private nature preserve and that's exactly what it was. There were acres and acres of woodlands and meadows and gardens. A crystal clear stream meandered lazily through one area and a small, spring-fed lake graced another. It was a beautiful place, full of wildlife and wonderful things to see and do. But sometimes, he felt very lonely. Like now.

Just then, out of the corner of his eye, Justin saw a movement at the window - a small flash of purple light. He jumped off the bed to get a closer look. The object flew to a bush several feet away. In the moonlight, Justin could see what appeared to be a small slender body with wings that sparkled. It must be a dragonfly, he thought. But dragonflies don't fly at night. They need warmth and sunlight. All at once, the small purple light pulsed brightly, then disappeared into the woods. Justin stared after it for a while until drowsiness overcame him. Crawling back into the snug cocoon of his blankets, he was soon fast asleep.

When he awoke, his memory of the mysterious purple object had vanished. After eating breakfast and helping his grandmother with some chores, he went for a walk. The sun was shining radiantly and everywhere he looked, there were birds and bees and butterflies busy with their daily activities. The ground was covered with wild violet blooms and dandelion blossoms and he stooped to pick some. They were his favorite flowers. He remembered the first time he picked a dandelion and violet bouquet for his mother. She had hugged him tight and told him he was her darling dear. Only his mother and grandmother called him that. Thinking about his mother now, made him miss her all the more and although he tried to fight it, he started to cry. Soon great big sloppy tears gushed out of his eyes and down his cheeks. They dripped off the edge onto his new shirt. And his nose ran. Oh how it ran, with each choking sob. He rubbed his eyes and nose on his shirt sleeves. He was quite a mess but he didn't care. All he cared about was seeing his mother. Seeing her sweet smile, having her rumple his hair and call him her 'darling dear', like she always did. Thinking of this made the tears come faster, harder - made his sobs louder. He plopped down on a large oak tree root and buried his head in his arms.

"I say - what's all the commotion? What's all the racket?" A deep booming voice bellared over Justin's sobs.

Startled, he jerked his tear-streaked face up and looked quickly around. "Where are you?" he asked. "*Who* are you?"

"I'm Grand Oak. That's who I am," came a deep indignant voice. "And I'm right here. You're sitting on one of my feet in fact, and I would like it if you would kindly *get off*. I have an ingrown root on that one and it hurts fiercesome when anything touches it."

16

Justin jumped up rubbing his eyes, rubbing his nose on his shirt again. He stared at the tree, long and hard. Then he saw!

"What are you staring at boy? Hasn't anyone told you it's not polite to stare? Haven't you ever seen a tree before?"

Justin stepped back a bit. He could see clearly now. The tree had two eyes and a mouth - a big mouth. And while the words coming out of it seemed grumbly, Justin could tell the eyes were kind and warm.

"Well, haven't you boy?" the tree boomed. "Seen a tree before, I mean?"

"Well, of course I have," Justin stammered. "But none that ever talked. None with eyes and a mouth!"

"Tut, tut, tut! We *all* have eyes and mouths. We all talk! We all think!" the tree scolded. "You humans are so full of yourselves. You like to believe you're the only ones who do! *Ha!* Fiddledee Spidget!"

"Fiddledee *what*?" Justin asked.

"Spidget! Spidget! You have wax buildup in your ears, boy?" the oak demanded.

"No! I've just never heard Fiddledee Spidget before, Grand Oak. What does it mean?"

"*Hogwash*, boy! That's what it means. Lots and lots of hogwash. Fallacy, untruth, figment of the imagination!! Get the picture?!

"Yes, yes, I do!" Justin said, feeling more than a little intimidated. Then remembering his manners, he added, "Thank you for explaining it Grand Oak. And I'm sorry I sat on your sore toe - eh, root."

"*Umph!*" the Oak muttered in an embarrassed tone, shrugging his large limbs nervously and creating a breeze as the leaves began to shake and rustle. "Well, since we got that straightened out, maybe you ought to tell me what all the blubbering was about.

I dare say you've made a complete mess of yourself!"

Inspecting himself quickly, Justin could see that Grand Oak was right. His shirt was wet and soiled. "I miss my mother," Justin responded. "She and my father are gone for five months on missionary work." Gazing up from his dirty shirt he saw Grand Oak's eyes soften and grow misty.

"Well, I know how it feels to miss your mother." he mumbled. "Been missing mine for a hundred years. Blew down in a terrible storm not long after I sprouted. Never have gotten over it. But no sense blubbering about it. Won't bring mine back. Won't bring your's home any quicker!"

Just then, their conversation was interrupted by another sound. A soft, muffled sort of crying. Justin and Grand Oak exchanged puzzled glances. The old tree's eyes narrowed.

"What in the world is going on this morning? he bellared again. "Has the whole world gone sad or mad or what?! Wherever you are, whoever you are, come out where I can see you and *stop that infernal blubbering!*"

Pitter had awakened to find himself laying on a toadstool in the bright sunlight, his milkweed down pillow from home propped under his head. The heat and glare made him very uncomfortable. Seldom had he ever been awake in daylight hours. Squinting, he looked cautiously around and realized this was the same woodland he always ended up in when he went sleep-flying. What a beautiful place - much more beautiful than The Golden Valley! Thinking of The Golden Valley, let loose a flood of upsetting images. The events of the night before came rushing back. The anguish in his mother's eyes, the disappointment in his grandfather's. He raised his left hand and looked at it. The multicolored Circles of Attunement stared back at him - a silent reminder of all the many ways he had let his family down. Perhaps everyone would be better off if he never went back. But what about his mother? He already missed her terribly. Could he really not go back? Not see her again? He didn't realize he had started to cry until the loud, booming voice broke through his thoughts. He could tell it was coming from a venerable old oak tree. Fairies know these things. His troubles temporarily forgotten, Pitter decided to show himself. Maybe the old oak could tell him about this place.

Grand Oak and Justin waited. They were aware that the crying had stopped. Just a tiny sniffle could be heard - a soft sniffle that seemed to move around a large bush and then in front of it. But Grand Oak and Justin saw nothing.

"I told you to show yourself!" Grand Oak ordered. "I demand to see you this minute!"

"I'm right in front of you," Pitter replied. "Look down, you silly old oak?"

"Oh my!" Grand Oak blustered excitedly, completely forgetting about Justin, who seemed frozen in stunned silence. "A fairy boy!" Oh my, oh my! You're a fairy boy! It has been years and years since this place had any fairies. Where did you come from? Where are your people? How did you get here? Are you staying? Are there others?" The questions tumbled out of Grand Oak like wild horses from a gate - running and bumping into each other. In fact, he was quite breathless when he finally stopped.

"It is obvious you are a wise and venerable oak," Pitter replied, having collected himself. "You know I cannot tell you where I came from. But I can tell you how I got here - sort of. I sleep-fly. It is a troublesome condition, I can't seem to control."

"Sleep-fly?!" Grand Oak asked uncertainly.

"Yes! explained Pitter. "Humans sometimes sleep-walk. But fairies, at least a few of us, sleep-*fly*!"

"Mercy me!" commiserated the old oak. "It must be a rare condition. I've never heard of such a thing before."

"It is quite rare," said Pitter. "No one else in our clan has it. I only wish I knew why I do."

All at once, Grand Oak remembered Justin, who was still standing, eyes wide, mouth gaping, in a state of shock. He nudged him with a lower branch.

"Mind your manners, boy and close your mouth." the old tree ordered. "You're in the presence of a *fairy boy!*"

"Where?" Justin asked eagerly. "I could hear him talking, but I can't see him."

Pitter darted a questioning look at Grand Oak.

"I see no harm," responded Grand Oak. "He's already partially sighted. He can see the *real* me."

Surprised and encouraged by this revelation, Pitter approached Justin and raised the wand which he had pulled from under his tunic. Then closing his eyes and tapping Justin's foot with it, he said, "Rays of sun and moonbeams bright, grant this mortal fairy sight."

A bright orange glow rose through Justin spreading from his feet to his legs and up and up until it reached the top of his head, then burst out and floated away. He blinked, then blinked again. Looking down, his eyes grew even wider than before with wonder. There standing in front of him was a fairy boy about four inches tall. He was dressed in a purple tunic tied at the waist with a gold cord. His feet were bare and he had a small pillow in one hand.

"I could have done that without the rhyme," the fairy told them smugly. "But I *love* rhymes!" "So, how does it feel being able to see a fairy, and what's your name?" he continued as he flew around Justin inspecting him.

"Amazing! Just amazing! And my name's Justin."

"You seem polite for a human," Pitter continued. "Not at all *neat,* but that's to be expected. Most humans aren't."

Justin looked down at his soiled shirt again, thought about explaining, and then decided against it. Instead, he asked, "What's your name?"

"Fairies never tell humans their names. You must guess or you will never know it. But I will give you a clue. What does rain sound like? Take your time for you are only allowed one guess."

"Pitter - Patter?"

"My, he is a quick one," Pitter said to Grand Oak with an admiring smile."

"So, your name is Pitter Patter, then?" Justin asked.

"No! Just one."

"Pitter?"

"Yes, yes! Jolly good! My twin brother is Patter - though I really shouldn't tell you that. A fairy's name is his own to share - no other's. But you would have figured it out, so no harm done. Besides, Patter is Momma's *good* boy. He wouldn't get angry or pull pranks on you anyway."

Justin stood silent, watching Pitter, wondering about the edge in his voice as he talked about his brother.

"Why aren't you talking? Asking me questions?" Pitter demanded. "Humans never stop talking and asking questions." Pitter could feel his impatient side starting to get the best of him.

"Well, I really don't think I should pry. Grandmother says it isn't polite."

Pitter clapped his hands together, spun around twice and then darted to and fro through the air coming to rest on a branch right in front of Justin's nose. "Oak, I dare say we have a treasure here. A human who respects people's privacy. I wonder how long it will last," he mused, rubbing his chin thoughtfully, his eyes growing dark and cold. "Perhaps, I shall have to test you someday" Pitter cautioned with a threatening tone in his voice. "Be forewarned!

I told you my brother is the *good* one!"

Without a word, Justin turned abruptly and started to walk away, back up the woodland path.

Stunned, Pitter raced after him swooping and diving in front of him. "Where are you going? Why are you leaving? We just met!"

"I don't mean to be rude," Justin said. "But I don't think I like you or your attitude. Taunting me. Saying mean things. At school we call people like you bullies!"

Pitter skidded to a stop in midair - hovering. Not until last night had anyone ever talked to him this way. His grandmother and mother and some of the others had hinted at such things, but never said them. It was not the fairy way. Instead, they said, 'Pitter you have much to learn before you can be King.' In the Land of Faerie in The Golden Valley, they called him 'the Charmer', 'the Prankster', but certainly not a bully!"

He had never really known a human boy. It might be fun to have one as a friend. And this one was 'sighted' now. What would his mother say if she found out he had given a human boy the gift of Fairy Sight and then alienated him? And she would *know*. She always *knew*! His mother had the gift of Glamour, something that still alluded him - among other things. Perhaps he did have a lot to learn. Maybe, in some way, this human boy could help him.

"You're right!" he apologized. "My behavior was inexcusable. Sometimes I think a wicked witch cursed my birth and gave me human manners. No offense!" he added quickly. "But most humans are quite impolite. And sometimes, I am more like them than the gentle folk. Can we start over? I would like to be friends. Tell you what. I'll prove it. Ask me anything. *Anything*! I promise I won't punish you or mischief you in any way. I give you my permission to pry." And he bowed a sweeping bow as he hovered in front of Justin's nose.

Justin couldn't help himself. He started to giggle. Then, so did Pitter. Soon they were both laughing so hard that they fell down on the ground rolling in the grass in a fit of uncontrollable laughter. When they finally stopped, they were exhausted.

"I meant what I said." Pitter said earnestly. "Ask me anything. Some things I can't tell you because it violates the Faerie Code, but if it is within my power to share, I will."

"Why were you crying?" Justin asked, taking Pitter at his word.

"I was missing my mother. Why were you crying?"

"I was missing my mother and father. What about *your* father?"

"I don't have one. Well, I did, but he passed on."

"Passed on? Fairies die?"

"They don't *die*. They *pass on* - to the Other Realm."

"Oh! Why did he pass on, if you don't mind my asking."

"Trying to fly in a rainstorm at night. See these wings," Pitter said, turning around and spreading them out for a good look. "They are sometimes much more handsome than they are functional. This delicate gossamer weaving won't stand up to things like bright sunshine or heavy rain. That's why I'm staying in the shade. My father crashed. Nothing could save him." A look of profound sadness spread across Pitter's face.

"Why was he flying in a rainstorm?"

"He was trying to get help for a lost child - a human child he found in the forest. It's a long sad story."

"He should have hitched a ride on an owl. They're great night fliers."

"I never thought of that! But come to think of it, there are no owls where we live. Haven't been for years."

"Well, there are around here." Justin said, turning Pitter's attention away from his father. "Would you like to meet one?"

"Sure," said Pitter enthusiastically.

"But what about the sun and your wings? We have to walk across the meadow where there is no shade to get to the Old Forest."

"No problem." Pitter said. And he flitted off among the trees bordering the path. Justin followed and watched as Pitter landed in front of a large colony of mayapples. Touching his wand to one, he chanted, "Flower of woodland, leaf of shade; may I take you from this glade?"

Justin watched in amazement as the leaf seemed to dip in a consenting bow toward Pitter. Pitter gently broke the leaf off from its stem, being careful not to disturb the delicate white flower hidden underneath. Then holding the leaf aloft over him like a large umbrella, he rejoined Justin.

"One should always ask before taking." he said. "And I like to do it with a rhyme. I love rhymes! Did I tell you that?"

"Yes, earlier." Justin replied.

Justin could just imagine what a strange sight they made as they crossed the meadow. Pitter alternately walked and flew with the large mayapple leaf waving merrily overhead. And all along the way he couldn't quit talking. He was so surprised at the variety of wild plants and grasses growing in the meadow. Every now and then he would have to stop and talk to particular plants that caught his attention. There were so many that he had not seen in years. He could hardly contain his excitement. This was a rare, fascinating place.

"I suppose you think it strange that I talk to plants?" he asked Justin.

"No!" Justin replied. "My grandmother does too. Sometimes, I do."

"*Really*?!" Pitter marveled.

"Yes. My grandmother believes that every plant has a spirit just like we do. And feelings."

"*Really*?!" Pitter said again. "So, just where did she get these ideas? It's certainly not common thinking among humans!"

"When she visited the Findhorn Gardens in Scotland. The people who started it were able to talk to the plant spirits. Because of that, they were very successful in growing plants where no one thought anything should grow. Seeing what had happened there, convinced my grandmother that plants are very much like people."

"Your grandmother must be very extraordinary."

Justin hadn't thought about it quite that way before, but hearing this, he knew it was true. "Yes, she is!" he said proudly.

"Is she a Sighted One?" Pitter asked.

"You mean, can she see fairies? I don't know!" Justin said, shrugging his shoulders.

"Bet she is!" Pitter chimed in. "We will know soon enough!"

"How?"

"A Sighted One is always able to recognize another. When you see each other next, you will both know if you both have the gift. Wait and see!"

By now they had reached the deep shade of the Old Forest. Pitter laid the mayapple leaf gently on the ground, then very reverently said, "Return to the soil, return to the earth; return to the mother who gave you birth." Then flitting playfully around Justin's head, he added, "I love rhymes! Did I tell you that?"

"Yes." Pitter answered. "You told me."

"So where is this owl?" Pitter asked as they trudged deeper into the dense Old Forest.

"We're almost there."

"This is a very ancient, very sacred place." Pitter said in an awed voice, looking around. He closed his eyes and breathed in deeply through his nose. Justin could see his tiny nostrils twitch and the most serene smile spread over his face. "I can't believe it," he said at last. "This is an old growth realm. The Elders live here."

"Elders?"

"Yes, very old fungi that live in the soil and provide the means for everything to grow. Humans don't understand how vital The Elders are. If they did, they wouldn't keep destroying them."

"How do you know they're here?"

"The smell. It's unmistakable if you know what to sniff for. Fairies think it is the sweetest fragrance in all the world. It's the aroma of life"

"Why can't I smell it?"

"Maybe you can. Problem is, most humans' noses have been so damaged by the bad air they breathe in cities that their sense of smell is only half what it should be. Perhaps you're different. Close your eyes and do just as I say. Make yourself relax completely. Push all the air out of your lungs. Now, concentrate all your thoughts on the little receptors in your nose. Very slowly, start breathing in through your nose. Invite the air in. Let it flow gently, slowly, from the front to the back, then into your lungs. Keep breathing in, taking the air up and up into your nose until your chest is full. Hold it a second. Concentrate only on the aromas. Now slowly let the air out. What did you smell?"

Justin stood transfixed, his eyes still closed. "Well, a lot of things. First, there was a deep musty smell like old decaying tree stumps. But then there seemed to be a mixture of other smells like warm sunshine and cool rain and blooming flowers and autumn leaves. It was a heavy, earthy smell, but it was very pleasant and very - *sweet*. You're right! It is the *sweetest* smell!

"You are amazing for a human," Pitter said. "Now that you have experienced the smell of The Elders, you will never forget it."

A loud 'who, who?' interrupted their conversation. Looking up, they saw a large, formidable looking owl sitting on a thick branch high above them. He blinked his eyes, then covered his mouth with the tip of his wing to stifle a gaping yawn. "Don't you know it's daytime, boys?" he asked in an annoyed voice. "Some of us are trying to sleep." Then taking a long second look at the pair below, he almost lost his balance. Gathering his wits about him, he took a third, even longer look. "Bless my feathers," he proclaimed excitedly. "Justin, you have a fairy boy with you! Where did you find a fairy boy? I can't even remember how long it's been since fairies lived in these parts?"

"This is Pitter, Owl. He wanted to meet you." Justin answered.

"Well, I'm most delighted to make your acquaintance, Pitter." the owl, said as he made a sweeping bow and almost toppled off the limb again. "But, I thought fairies only came out at night - like owls. It's daylight. You should be asleep. Come to think of it, I should be asleep."

"I usually am." agreed Pitter. "But I have a bad habit of sleep-flying and happened to end up here. And there has been so much to see and do since I woke up, that I completely forgot how tired I am." The tingling of a bell in the distance interrupted.

"Ah," said Owl. "It's Justin's lunch time. Grandmother is summoning you home for, no doubt, another delectable repast. How I sometimes wish my intestinal tract was designed to accommodate her culinary wonders. A most talented woman, your grandmother. You mustn't keep her waiting."

"I know," said Justin. "You won't leave will you, Pitter?"

"Well, not for a while. I think I'll stay right here with Owl and take a long nap. I'll tell you what." After the moon rises tonight, look for me out your bedroom window where you saw me early this morning."

The memory of the purple object popped back in Justin's mind. "That was you?" he asked.

"Yes. What did you think it was? A dragonfly?"

The bell rang again. Reluctantly Justin said goodbye to Owl and Pitter and scurried off in its direction.

Chapter Three

Grandmother was just putting a small vase of violets and dandelions on the table when Justin hurried in. She looked up at his flushed, eager face and knew at once that something was different. She studied him a second. Could it be?

"I found these scattered on the garden path this morning after you left for your walk," she said. "They were beginning to wilt, but I got them into water just in time. I thought you must have picked them since you love them so."

"Yes, I did." Justin answered. "But then things happened and I must have dropped them."

"What things?" Grandmother asked. She was eying him closely now, sure the signs were there.

Justin was watching her carefully too. He could see it now. A look about his grandmother he had never quite noticed before. Like a presence or an aura - something he couldn't describe but was very aware of. It must be what Pitter meant about recognizing a Sighted One.

"Oh, you darling dear," his grandmother exclaimed, running over and enveloping him in her arms. "This must mean there's a fairy here. At *long last*! And it has given you the gift of full sight." She was overwhelmed with joy. She grabbed Justin's hands and began to sing and dance around the room, bumping into the chairs and the table. Only when the shrill sound of the teakettle whistle drowned out their merry tune, did they fall into their chairs in a state of helpless laughter.

"You must tell me everything." Grandmother said, as she busied herself about the kitchen brewing the tea and filling their plates. And without any further coaxing, Justin told her about his eventful morning.

When the moon rose that night, Justin was anxiously waiting on a stool in front of his bedroom window. Over and over, his gaze skimmed the bushes and tree tops outside. What if Pitter had decided to go home? What if he never came again? There were so many things Justin wanted to show him and ask him. Most of all, he and his grandmother wanted Pitter to stay. The gardens and the woodlands needed fairies. The plant spirits always responded better to fairies, than to humans. As beautiful as the gardens and woodlands were now, they would be even more spectacular if there were fairies about.

Justin waited and waited. The moon rose higher and higher in the sky and his eyelids grew heavier and heavier. He didn't realize he had fallen asleep until he was startled by tapping on the windowpane. Rubbing the sleep from his eyes, he burst into a smile. There was Pitter at last. He hadn't left after all. Justin started to raise the window so he could talk to his new friend, but instantly Pitter flashed right through the glass and landed on Justin's shoulder.

"Sorry I'm late." he apologized. "Can you believe? I overslept! Don't know the time I've ever done that. Must be from being awake half the day. You didn't give up, did you?"

"Well, sort of." Justin said.

"A fairy's word is his bond." Pitter said fervently. "Know

this always. If a fairy tells you something, it is true. As sure as the sky is blue. Hey, that's almost a rhyme. Did I tell you I like rhymes?"

"I think so." Justin answered, knowing that Pitter had, but not wanting to offend him by reminding him of how many times.

"So, is she? Your grandmother? Is she a Sighted One?"

"Yes."

"I knew it! *I knew it*! This is truly an awesome place. Can you show me around some more tomorrow?"

"You're staying?"

"Well, at least for a day or two. I'd like to learn a little more about everything here. Maybe, I'll find out why I always end up here when I sleep-fly."

"Then I'll be happy to show you around. Would you like to meet my grandmother?"

"Not just yet. One human at a time is quite enough - no offense. Of course, it makes a difference that you're sighted. And I must ask your grandmother about all of this sometime. But not right away."

Justin yawned feeling the drowsiness creeping back into his body. Then Pitter yawned too. "I must be getting adjusted to human ways." he said. "After being up most of the night and day, I'm ready to go back to sleep again. Seems strange to sleep in the dark. See you in the morning!" And with that, Pitter disappeared through the window glass and off into the distant forest.

Relieved to know his new friend would still be around in the morning, Justin went to sleep.

Breakfast was already on the table when Justin awoke. He hadn't slept that soundly since his parents left. Of course he still missed them, but it was very nice not to stay awake half the night wondering about them. As he expected, his grandmother was full of questions. He told her all about Pitter's brief evening visit. She was as thrilled as Justin was, that Pitter had decided to stay a day or two. Perhaps, he would become attached to this special place and end up making it his permanent residence. They could only hope. Grandmother was not at all upset, as Justin feared she might be, that Pitter had not wanted to meet her just yet. In fact, she echoed Pitter's own remark, that it was probably enough to deal with one human at a time. He was seeing facets of his grandmother that he had never known existed and he felt very lucky.

After dishes and chores, Justin headed off for the Old Forest. He was sure he would find Pitter there, if Pitter wanted to be found. Or perhaps Pitter would find him first. The sun was shining brightly and although it was still early morning, the heat was intense. Justin patted his pocket and wondered what Pitter would think of the present his grandmother had made for him. He didn't have to wonder very long. Just as he entered the shade of the Old Forest and started to breathe in the smell of The Elders, a flash of purple light swooped down and tickled his nose.

"I thought you were going to sleep all day!" Pitter declared. "I've been waiting since sun up."

"I had chores to do and then Grandmother wanted me to wait while she finished a present for you."

"A present? For me? Oh, you humans can be a delight! I love presents! Where is it? What is it?'"

Justin reached in his pocket, pulled out a small package and handed it to Pitter. Pitter grinned with pleasure and unwrapped it. "What is this?" he asked puzzled. "It looks like a pair of wings about my size. And they appear to be made out of lamb's ears leaves."

"Yes, you're right. If you look closely, each wing consists of two lamb's ears leaves sown together. Grandmother thought you could slip these over your own wings to protect them from the sun."

"What a thoughtful thought!" Pitter exclaimed. "I think she may have something here. Let's give them a try."

Justin knelt down on the ground behind Pitter. Standing stiff and straight, his arms crossed over his chest, legs wide apart, Pitter flexed his shoulders, spreading out his wings while Justin slipped the lamb's ears sheaths over each one.

"How do they feel?"

"Soft! Light! Wonderful!" Pitter replied as he flew around Justin testing them. "This is perfect. I can follow you anywhere without having to worry about the sun. I must remember to do something very nice for your grandmother! But come with me. I have something to show you. I've been exploring."

The two companions headed off deeper and deeper into the Old Forest. They were careful not to talk too loudly for fear of waking Owl. Both felt it wouldn't be wise to disturb his sleep two days in a row. At last Pitter stopped and beamed at Justin.

"Look at this!" he exclaimed with delight, pointing to a large expanse of rich green leaves covering the forest floor.

"Yes, goldenseal." Justin said matter-of-factly.

"You know this plant?"

"Of course. My grandmother and I planted a thousand rootlets in the woods on the other side of the meadow a couple of weeks ago. Grandmother has brought me to this spot lots of times. She said these plants have been here for many years. We are extremely careful not to let anyone else know about them or they would probably be gone."

"They *are* gone in The Golden Valley - completely. We haven't seen any in our woodlands for many years. I can't believe there is so much of it here. This is rare. Very rare. And look over here."

"Yes, American ginseng."

"You know it too?"

"Of course. We also planted a thousand rootlets of it in the woods. But these have been here, Grandmother says, since she was a girl. And over there is bloodroot, and trout lily, and lady's slipper, and Virginia bluebells, and wild ginger, and . . ."

"Wild ginger? Where? I didn't see *it*. Oh, I think I'll burst like a jewelweed pod! I *love* wild ginger meat and I haven't had any for years and years. Ginger meat is my favorite treat! Hey, that rhymes. I suppose I told you I love rhymes?"

"Yes, I think you did."

Pitter knelt down near the colony of wild ginger and politely asked the plant for its permission to take a piece of its root. The plant nodded in agreement and very gently, Pitter scooped the rich humus away and exposed a large knobby root. Then he tapped it with his wand and a small piece fell off. Tapping again, the clean cut wound on the remainder of the root sealed over. Pitter carefully covered the root again and pressed the soil firmly around it. All the while, he hummed a sweet melody. Then he rejoined Justin, holding his prize.

"I've never heard such a tune before." Justin said.

"It's a harvesting song." Pitter explained. "It is meant to soothe the plant and thank it at the same time. Too often humans take without thinking or showing any appreciation for the gift the plant is giving. This is a terrible mistake - one fairies never make."

"What are you going to do with your piece of wild ginger?"

"Put it in my secret pouch so I can savor its goodness later."

"Where's your secret pouch?"

"Here." Pitter reached under his tunic and pulled out a small silver bag tied with golden string. He opened it.

"But that won't fit in there." Justin protested.

"Yes it will. Watch." Pitter said. With that he raised the piece of ginger to the small opening in the top of the silver pouch.

Immediately the ginger compressed into a tiny nugget and dropped into the bag. Pitter laughed at the look of surprise on Justin's face. "There are definite advantages to being a fairy, wouldn't you say?"

"Yes." Justin agreed.

"By the way," Pitter continued, motioning toward the backpack Justin was wearing.. "I meant to ask, what's in your bag."

"Oh, I forgot! Grandmother made us a picnic lunch."

"Umm!" Pitter said. "This should be interesting. I'll be quite curious to see what she sent us when it comes time to eat. Where will we eat this 'picnic'?"

"I thought you might like to see the lake. It's in the woods across the meadow. There are ducks there and turtles and frogs. I love frogs. The lake is my favorite place."

"Well, then that's just where we shall go. I would like to see your favorite place. And I have a special fondness for frogs myself. I've seen lots of tree frogs here in the Old Forest, but I really like bullfrogs. Of course, since most of them are bigger than I am, I have to be careful around them. They would never mean to hurt me but they are quite heavy and clumsy sometimes, and very quick if they're startled. Have you ever seen a fairy ride a frog? Well, of course, you haven't! But maybe today. Maybe today!"

Justin was so intent on trying to picture Pitter riding a bullfrog that he stumbled over a large root and almost fell down. At the last second, he felt a tug on the backpack that stopped his fall. Looking around, he saw Pitter hovering behind him with a smug look on his face.

"The least I could do." Pitter said.

It took them longer than Justin had planned to reach the lake in the woods. All the way across the meadow, Pitter had to stop to talk to plants and bees and birds and butterflies. Here and

35

there he would find an old plant friend that he hadn't seen in years and he would spend even more time renewing acquaintances. It wasn't any different once they left the meadow and entered the woods. Every step along the way, Pitter marveled at the abundance and diversity of the plant families he encountered. Justin couldn't help being overwhelmed with pride that his fairy friend was so impressed. When they finally arrived at the lake, the sun was high overhead and Justin's stomach was rumbling with hunger.

"Would you like to eat now?" Justin asked, fervently hoping Pitter was as hungry as he was. He assumed fairies experienced hunger.

"Yes, I believe I would." Pitter replied. "More to satisfy my curiosity about what your grandmother packed, than my hunger. Fairies don't get hungry like humans."

"I was wondering about that." Justin admitted.

"We can live on very little." Pitter explained. "A little rose dew, a few marshmallow cheeses, a nibble of watercress, a pinch or two of seeds. It doesn't take much. So what do you have for us in that contraption on your back?"

"Well, I don't think there is anything in here that you mentioned. Grandmother said she has always read that fairies like bread and milk." His face fell as he saw Pitter wrinkle his nose up with disdain at the mention of milk. "You don't like milk?"

"Sorry. Humans have mistakenly thought that for far too long. Fairies find milk most distasteful. It must be the smell. Yes, I think it's the smell. Imagine the delicate aroma of flower dew and how sweet it must taste. Then, think of how milk *smells*!" Pitter shivered at the thought and wrinkled his nose again in disgust.

"Well, the dew is dry on the plants now, but we could get some fresh water from the spring over there. Grandmother calls *it*, 'the nectar of the gods'. Maybe you would like it."

"Yes. That sounds much better. Now, what about this bread

you mentioned?"

"Grandmother said to tell you it is made from spring water, whole wheat, honey, and anise, and leavened with wild yeast!"

"Now there is a treat almost equal to my piece of wild ginger. What are we waiting for?"

Pleased that Pitter approved of his grandmother's bread, Justin hurriedly opened his backpack and began laying out its contents. Respecting his friend's feelings, he left the thermos of milk inside. There were slices of the bread along with homemade peanut butter and black raspberry jelly. A container of fresh strawberries from the garden and homemade oatmeal cookies rounded out the meal. Pitter decided to sample a little of everything. He was most curious about the peanut butter. Remembering Pitter's mention of eating only very small amounts of food, Justin put a tiny portion of each on a small plate and handed it to Pitter. Pitter looked it over, then set it down on the ground in front of where he was sitting.

"Is something wrong?" Justin asked.

"No. I just can't eat when I'm holding my plate." With that he extended the slender fingers on his left hand toward the peanut butter. Then holding out his right hand, palm up, he extended the fingers of his left hand toward his palm. Justin watched in rapt fascination as a small pile of tiny golden nuggets appeared in Pitter's outstretched palm. He thought his eyes would pop out of his head when a second later the small pile disappeared as if by magic.

"Where did it go?"

"Inside."

"Inside? But how can that be?"

"Fairies don't eat with their mouths like humans. It's so messy, so uncivilized. We absorb our food through our skin, except for drinkable things. Those we like to sip. It's much more refined than all that chewing and smacking. No offense! I know you don't

37

have any choice but to eat like a human. Pity!"

Justin hesitated. He felt a little self-conscious now about eating, but he was very hungry. And he knew his skin wasn't going to help him fill his stomach. So, trying to be as quiet and neat as possible, he started to eat. He was aware that Pitter had averted his eyes. He wondered if Pitter thought it was the polite thing to do or if he was just too repulsed to look. Feeling increasingly uncomfortable, he ate quickly, being ever so careful not to smack his lips or slop food on his shirt. When he finished, he started to pack the things away, then realized that Pitter's plate was still full.

"But I thought you ate everything." Justin said.

"I did, and it was quite delightful, I must say. My compliments to your grandmother."

"But your plate is still full."

"No it isn't." Pitter countered. "Oh! You think because the shapes are still there that the food is there? Another mistake humans make. I don't know how many times since the beginning of humans that little children have cried with disappointment because they think the fairies haven't eaten the food they set out for them. Fairies don't have space inside for foods like you do. Remember the little pile of golden nuggets in my hand?"

"Yes."

"That was the food's goodness. That's all we eat. We pull the goodness from the foods through our finger tips - the shape remains. Fairies aren't made like human's you know."

"I know. But this is something really new. I don't remember ever hearing anything about this before. Neither has my grandmother."

"You think because we look much like humans that our forms work the same way. This is another misconception humans have. Every living thing has a spirit that is at the core of its existence. The spirit is the same in everything, only the form given by the Creator is different. Every living thing is assigned a different purpose and the form must facilitate the accomplishment of that purpose. It is all part of The Great Master Plan. Fairies look much like humans because we are the liaisons between humans and the natural kingdom. Since we must, from time to time, communicate with humans, we need to have a form acceptable to them. But much of our form is more sophisticated than yours. No offense."

"Well, if you need to look like humans so you can talk to us without scaring us, why are you so little?"

"Humans would feel intimidated by us if we were the same size they are. Think of it. If I were exactly the same size you are and yet had the same powers I do, wouldn't you find that a little frightening?"

"Yes."

"Of course, we weren't always *this* small."

"Really?"

"Yes, back when the First People arrived, we were about half as tall as you are now."

"So, why did you shrink?"

"It's a disturbing trend that has been happening slowly over the last five-hundred human years. We live totally in tune with the environment. We are dependent on it for our survival. Over the years, The Elders in the forest have been destroyed, causing a loss of the nutrients we need. The waters have become fouled with harmful elements. The air is heavy with chemicals. The soils are depleted and toxic. Humans get sick and die. Fairies quit growing and shrink. The problem is so widespread, that there seems to be no way to stop it. Too few listen. Even fewer act. Our fear now is that some day, we will all be gone. All of us. Fairies and humans alike."

Justin sat frozen is silence mulling over these somber, ominous words. He knew it was true and he felt very small and

helpless. A loud splash broke the heavy silence and Pitter and Justin looked up just in time to see a brightly colored drake dive underwater.

"So much for gloom and doom." Pitter said, jumping up. "If fairies know one thing, it's how to make the best of the present moment. In the end, it's really all any of us have. I see a fat bullfrog on that lily pad over there," he said, pointing. "Would you like to see me ride him?"

"Oh, yes!" Justin exclaimed with excitement. "I only wish I could give it a try too!"

"Umm."

Justin watched as Pitter untied the cord around his waist. Then flexing his lamb's ears encased wings, he flew over toward the lily pad. The slumbering frog was totally oblivious to the small fairy hovering over him. Seizing the moment, Pitter quickly dropped from the air and came to rest on the frog's back. In a flash, he looped the cord under the bullfrog's fat neck. Instantly, the frog was awake and aware of pressure on his back. Instinctively he leaped into the water and dove. Pitter held on for dear life, forcing his eyes to stay open so he could enjoy the show. Startled tadpoles whizzed by. Bits of moss and fragments of leaves whipped around them. Still deeper and deeper the frog dove, twisting and turning, trying in vain to rid himself of his unwanted passenger. Pitter hung on. Hitting bottom, the frog pushed off with his powerful legs and soared upward. Faster and faster he went. The light was rushing up to meet them. With a resounding pop, they broke the surface. So strong was the frog's momentum, that frog and fairy were airborne for several feet, flying in an arch through the air over the open water. With a loud splash, they entered the water again. Exhausted, the frog swam to the edge of the lake just in front of where Justin was standing doubled over with laughter. All around the quiet lake, rabbits and squirrels and deer and other woodland creatures peered out from their hiding places to see what all the commotion was about. With a look of defeat in his eyes, the large frog, with Pitter still on his back, crawled slowly up the bank. Pitter wiped the water from his eyes, the moss out of his hair. His tinkling laughter filled the air like a thousand tiny bells. Retrieving the cord from around the bullfrog's neck he slid down and patted him on the rump.

"Thank you for the invigorating ride. You have remarkable swimming skills my green friend."

"No wonder!" said the frog, in a deep raspy voice. "I should have known it was a fairy. Nothing else could best me like that. Never gave it a thought though. Haven't been fairies around since my great, great grandpappy was a tadpole. You stayin'?"

"Maybe." Pitter replied.

Justin smiled inside as the implications of that 'maybe' darted around in his mind. So there was hope. Pitter hadn't said 'no' this time. Only 'maybe'.

Quite weary now from providing the afternoon's entertainment, the bullfrog excused himself and went back to rest on his lily pad. "That was the *best* fun!." Pitter exclaimed. "Riding bullfrogs is one of my favorite things to do at home. My grandfather doesn't approve. Patter would never do such a thing, but I think it is incredible fun. The bullfrogs don't mind, so I say no harm's done."

"It really does look like awesome fun." Justin agreed. "Scary - but awesome! I wish I could see what it feels like to ride a bullfrog to the bottom of the lake and back.

"I wish you could too." Pitter said, his voice tinged with disappointment. If my mother was here, she could make it so. She has the power to shape-shift; make things different shapes and sizes. Most fairies do. Grandfather says the power alludes me because I'm not responsible enough to know how to use it properly. If I could shape-shift, I could make you small enough to ride that bullfrog.

But I can't." A look of sadness spread over Pitter's face.

Justin searched his brain for a way to change the subject. Just then, he noticed something that should do the trick. The lamb's ears sheaths protecting Pitter's delicate, shimmering wings were gone.

"Your wings!" Justin said pointing to Pitter's back. "They're exposed. The coverings must have come off in the water."

Pitter hadn't noticed either that they were missing until now. "I guess, we'll have to stay in the shade." he said. "Perhaps your grandmother could make me another pair for tomorrow."

"So," Justin asked expectantly as they sought out a shady spot under a group of sprawling oaks and maples. "You plan to be here tomorrow. You aren't going home just yet?"

Pitter's eyes clouded over briefly. Justin couldn't tell if it was from anger or sadness.

"I'll stay at least another day or two. Then we'll see."

Justin was feeling quite tired from all the excitement and sprawled on the soft grass. Pitter gazed around until he spied a soft bed of lush green moss. "Moss is my favorite thing to lay on," he explained. "Grass tickles." Reaching under his tunic, he pulled out the silver pouch and after searching through its contents, retrieved a tiny rectangular object. He placed it on a leaf, then tapped it with his wand. Immediately, it became larger and Justin recognized it as the pillow Pitter had with him when they first met at the base of Grand Oak.

"I didn't realize fairies used pillows like ours."

"Well we do and we don't. Mine probably isn't *just* like your's. Spiders taught the Ancient Ones how to spin milkweed down into cloth many years ago. My mother made the pillow casing from the milkweed cloth made by the fairy weavers, then she filled it with milkweed down and sweet grass. With this, I never fail to get a good day's sleep. Although, my sleep patterns are certainly mixed up now, and a good *night's* sleep would be more fitting to say." Once again, Pitter reached into the silver pouch. This time, he pulled out the piece of shriveled wild ginger. A tap and it was restored to normal too. With his finger tips, Pitter extracted some golden nugget goodness, then watched with pleasure as it disappeared through his skin. "Yum!" he exclaimed with satisfaction. "Now that is truly delicious." Adjusting the pillow on the moss, he rested his head on it and gazed up at the tree tops high above. What a peaceful, beautiful place this was.

Watching quietly, Justin remembered something Pitter had said when they were in the Old Forest. He had wondered about it at the time but hesitated to ask. Now his curiosity got the best of him. "When we were in the Old Forest and found the wild ginger," he began, "You said you hadn't seen any in years and years. What did you mean? I figure you must be about my age. You look like you are. But now I'm not sure that anything is like I think it is. How old are you?"

"Ah, ha!" Pitter exclaimed cheerfully. "How old am I? Considerably older than you."

"But you don't look older."

"Fairy time and human time are not at all the same. Fairies are on the earth much, much longer than humans."

"How long?"

"Well, for instance, you know the story of that Columbus fellow who gets the credit for discovering America? What a laugh!"

"Yes, I know the story. What about it?"

"Well, Grandmother says that was the same year my mother was born."

Justin sat up with a jolt. Quickly he calculated the numbers in his mind, his eyes growing wider and wider."

"You mean - you mean - your mother is over 500 years old?"

"Yes. Guess so!"

"Then how old are you?"

"Well, not quite that old, certainly. But you see, in fairy time, I'm just now reaching what you humans call manhood."

Justin shook his head in disbelief. "So what else do you have in your silver pouch?" he asked.

Pitter flashed a wide grin and removed the pouch again from under his tunic. "Treasures!" he confided merrily, reaching inside. "Here's a small conch shell from the shores of The Great Sea. If you hold it up to your ear, you can hear the roaring of the mighty water spirits. It was my great-grandfather's." Pitter tapped the tiny object and it grew in size. He handed it to Justin. Holding it against his ear, Justin could, indeed, hear the sound of the ocean waves. He handed it back with an appreciative smile. One by one, Pitter extracted other cherished items - unique rocks, glittering gemstones, a pinch of real gold dust. It seemed impossible for so many things to fit in the little silver pouch. Of course, they wouldn't if they were stored while still their normal size.

"I thought you couldn't shape-shift." Justin commented.

"I can't - except for my food and my treasures!" Pitter could tell his new friend was growing weary and had absorbed all he could for one day. Yawning, he said. "Your grandmother is probably wondering about you. You look like you could use a nap, and I wouldn't mind a little snooze in Owl's tree myself.

"Yes. A nap does sound like a good idea." Justin agreed.

With a wave and a reminder about the lamb's ears wings, Pitter and Justin parted company. Justin was so tired when he got home that he couldn't even muster enough strength to tell his grandmother about his eventful day. The only information she could get out of him before he fell soundly off to sleep was that Pitter loved the bread, hated milk, and needed another pair of lamb's ears wings for tomorrow. That was really all she wanted to know. Pitter was staying -- at least for tomorrow.

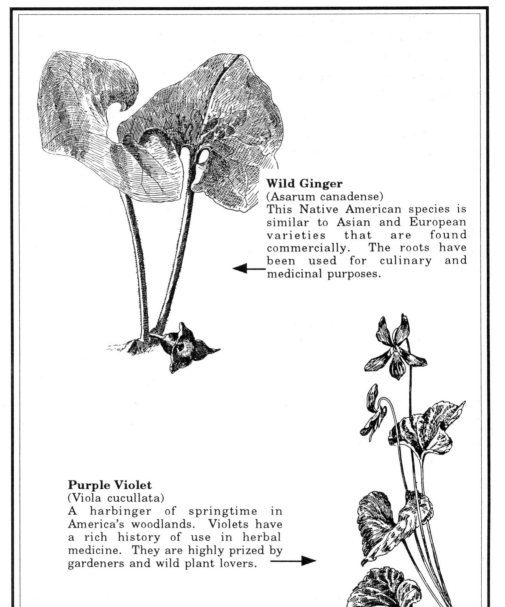

Wild Ginger
(Asarum canadense)
This Native American species is similar to Asian and European varieties that are found commercially. The roots have been used for culinary and medicinal purposes.

Purple Violet
(Viola cucullata)
A harbinger of springtime in America's woodlands. Violets have a rich history of use in herbal medicine. They are highly prized by gardeners and wild plant lovers.

Chapter Four

In The Golden Valley, fairy nurses were frantically working overtime. The King had been gravely injured on his way home from an evening of dancing the night before. It had started out as a splendid occasion. The woodlands had been aglow with the light of a full moon. A fairy had discovered a patch of new grass just at the edge of the woods. Dancers were summoned to test it. They found it extremely soft, with just the right amount of cushiness to put spring in even their most intricate steps. The King declared that all work should be suspended for the night and nothing but dancing and merriment be pursued. Absolutely no one objected. Lively music, soft chatter, and tinkling laughter filled the moonlit night.

Near dawn, the King had summoned his carriage and his hounds and everyone headed off to bed in good spirits. But on the way to the palace, the King's carriage hit a rock. The King, drowsy from all the merrymaking, was thrown out. His royal head hit a tree. It was obvious immediately that his injury was quite severe. He was quickly transported to the palace. Nurses were summoned and soon spread the word that his fate was beyond their powers to control. A somber vigil began.

The announcement of the King's accident and tragic condition reached Lyla and Patter as they were trying to cope with their own troubles. They assumed when they found Pitter gone the night before, that it was just another sleep-flying incident. The outer guards had reported they saw him leave. But he had not returned.

Rumors began to fly that Pitter had run away. Lyla and Patter had denied this but as the hours wore on, it became more and more difficult to defend him. The stress of worrying and wondering soon took its toll on Lyla. Fearful for her health, she was ordered to bed and put in the care of fairy nurses. Hour after hour they tended her with a mixture of flower essences collected in the evening dew. She drifted in and out of fitful sleep, crying out frequently for her darling dear Pitter.

A feeling of unease gnawed at Pitter as he rested on a branch in the Old Forest. Darkness had fallen only minutes before. Owl and the other nocturnal creatures of the forest had just left for their night of hunting. Aided by the brilliant light of a full moon, they should have much success. Pitter said a silent prayer for the plants and small animals that would sacrifice their lives to sustain their larger prey. It was the law of nature. It was the way the great Earth had been designed by the Creator to maintain balance. If only the humans had not thrown it out of kilter.

His thoughts turned to his own dilemma. He missed his mother and Patter and his grandmother. He missed the fairy kingdom. As much as he enjoyed Justin's company and wanted to learn more about this place and his grandmother, Pitter knew he must go home. He was sure his mother was sick with worry. How could he keep her in a state of turmoil? And the King? Pitter had thought long and hard about his behavior since his father died. The King had been right to punish him. He *was* out of attunement. He owed his grandfather an apology - the sooner, the better.

Reminded now of the Circles, Pitter raised his hand to peer at them in the moonlight. He was astonished to see that two of them were gone. He must be seeing things! He blinked his eyes and looked more intently. Yes, two of them had definitely disappeared. His heart raced with excitement. He wondered what he had done to erase them. Only good thoughts and deeds could accomplish such a thing. Perhaps, befriending a human boy had done the trick. He would have to ask the King when he returned. He was resolved now. He must go back. But he couldn't leave without saying goodbye to Justin and meeting his grandmother. He would spend one more day. Then, tomorrow after darkness fell, he would force himself to go to sleep and will himself to return to The Golden Valley. Surely if he focused his powers hard enough, he could make it happen. He *must* make it happen!

He leaned his head back on his milkweed down pillow and closed his eyes. The night sounds filled his ears. Off in the distance owls hooted to each other against a medley of insect tunes and babble. Below, scurrying raccoons, deer, opossums and other animals rustled leaves and cracked twigs. Whip-poor-wills called soulfully for their mates. And the frogs, not to be outdone, croaked and sang, adding their own special touch to the harmonious blend. The sweet scent of The Elders mingled with that of thousands of spring blossoms and wafted over Pitter, soothing a strange sense of foreboding that tugged at him. His eyes closed and he drifted off.

Chapter Five

Pitter awoke to a world transformed. The comforting night sounds had been replaced by the raucous cries of crows, the cheery songs of robins and cardinals, the shrill squawks of blue jays, the incessant tapping of woodpeckers. Wasps and bees buzzed and everywhere baby birds could be heard chirping insistently for food. The moon had long disappeared, replaced by a brilliant, pulsating sun. How quickly the night had flown. Pitter was just tucking his pillow into his silver pouch when he heard a familiar voice calling his name. With a mixture of eagerness and sadness, he swooped down to join Justin.

"Grandma let me skip my chores this morning." Justin said, greeting his small friend. "And look. She sent along another pair of lamb's ears wings for you."

"Your grandmother is truly a special person." Pitter declared, turning to let Justin slip the grey velvet sheaths over his sun-sensitive wings. He wiggled briefly to adjust them just right.

"In fact, I would like to meet your grandmother." he added. "What is her name? No! Don't tell me. One's name is their own to share. It is at the core of their being and demands utmost respect. I must ask her myself."

"She would like that." Justin said. "When do you want to meet her?"

"It's not my way, to ever delay," Pitter answered. Then beaming with delight, he blurted. "I made a rhyme. How I love rhymes! Did you know that?"

"Yes," Justin answered, trying very hard not to show his impatience at Pitter's repetitious mention of this fact. "Grandma is working in the herb garden this morning," he continued. "If you'd like, you could meet her there.

"Perfect! Show the way!"

As they approached the herb garden, Pitter swooped up and whispered in Justin's ear. Obediently, Justin stretched his arms behind his back, cupping his hands. Pitter sat down in Justin's upturned palm and waited. Hands still behind his back, Justin pushed through the gate, whistling nonchalantly. His grandmother looked up and flashed him a welcoming smile. At her feet was her harvesting basket laden with lush sprigs of rosemary and thyme and basil. Their delicious aromas danced around them in the air.

"I didn't expect to see you again until late afternoon," she said.

"I have a surprise for you," Justin answered, unable to keep the excitement out of his voice.

A questioning look crossed her face and then was replaced with one of eager anticipation. Could it be? Yes, she felt it. Pitter was with him.

Pitter knew instantly that she was aware of his presence. He flitted up and stood on Justin's shoulders. Justin laughed and introduced them. What happened next caught him totally off guard. His grandmother melted in a heap on the ground crying. Never would he have dreamed this would happen., Forgetting Pitter, he rushed to her and tried to comfort her. She enveloped him in her arms, rocking back and forth. At last, her sobs subsided and she struggled to get control of herself. She hugged Justin tenderly, then stood up and looked around.

Pitter, had found himself a perch on a wide elecampane leaf and had watched all of this with interest. He had never encountered this reaction before. Granted, he had had little contact himself with humans, but this seemed to be a most unusual response. Undaunted, he decided to try again. Taking care not to startle her, he flew to a rosebush next to her, making sure he exuded enough purple light for her to spot and follow him as he flew. He landed on a lovely, cream-colored rose bud and slid down it to straddle the stem. He leaned his elbows on the bud and looked inquisitively at Justin's grandmother, then flashed his most charming smile. Back at The Golden Valley, he was famous for his charming smiles. Of course, some would snidely say he was *infamous* for them!.

To his delight, Justin's grandmother smiled back. Whatever had frightened or troubled her initially, seemed to have vanished. In no time, they were engrossed in lively conversation. It was readily apparent that Justin's grandmother had a special fondness for the herb garden and Pitter politely asked for a tour.

"But, before we continue," Pitter said. "I feel a bit uncomfortable calling you grandmother, since I have two grandmothers of my own. If you don't mind, I would be most honored to know your given name."

"Why, I'd be most honored to share it with you. My name is Faye."

"Faye," Pitter repeated, letting the sound of it spill enchantingly from his lips. "A lovely name, befitting even a fairy! Travelers from other lands have told us some humans used to call fairies, 'fays'. I am most honored to make your acquaintance, Faye!" he said, bowing deeply.

Faye curtsied and replied with a girlish giggle. "I am most humbled and delighted to make yours, Pitter."

With these formalities over, the three companions set off to explore the extensive herb garden. Pitter marveled at the vast array of plants. There were beautiful basils that he was familiar with and exotic new ones he had never seen. There were lush stands of mint and oregano and mounds of all different types of thyme. Pitter was particularly intrigued with a ground hugging, tiny leaved thyme.

"Maybe you would like to sleep here one night." Justin offered.

"Why?" Pitter asked, surprised at the suggestion.

"Fairies love to sleep in beds of thyme." Justin countered.

"Says who? Oh, you must be speaking of fairies who live across The Great Sea. Travelers have told us *they* like to sleep in beds of thyme. Never quite understood why. Now this little, soft flat one looks very comfortable, but others? No, not for me. I prefer sleeping in treetops where I know I won't be stepped on by a careless human. No offense! And on rare occasions, when I do sleep on the ground, I much prefer a bed of soft moss or milkweed down."

"Oh!" Justin and his grandmother exchanged glances. This was new to them and certainly contradicted what they had read. But looking first at Pitter and then at the beds of thyme, it was easy to see why sleeping in them might not be the most comfortable experience. Some of the woody stems would surely stick a fairy painfully here and there, and it was quite easy to imagine how the leaves could tickle. Yes, they could see Pitter's point. A bed of moss might be much more pleasing. That must be why some mosses are called fairy moss.

They moved on around the garden. Pitter spoke respectfully to each plant, eliciting a nod or a flutter as he passed by. Some he knew instantly, others he asked about. His delight in their beauty and function and fragrance was contagious. Justin found himself admiring each in a new way. To their surprise, he wasn't familiar with lavender or rosemary. "Few humans have ever lived in The Golden Valley," he explained. "And those who have, grew a limited number of herbs." Pitter's family knew and loved the wild things, but had little experience with plants cultivated in gardens. Besides, most herbs grown in gardens had been brought to this land from across The Great Sea - like the rosemary and lavender. Native fairies who spent their lives secluded in remote woodlands, had little opportunity to acquaint themselves with these newcomers.

Pitter was intrigued with the rosemary. Faye gave him a sprig from her harvesting basket and he immediately twined it into a circle and placed it on his head, sniffing the air and his hands as he did so, reveling in its fragrance.

"It's interesting that you should do that." Faye said.

"Why?"

"Rosemary has a long history of being called 'the herb of remembrance'. Hundreds of years ago, people made crowns of it to wear on their heads to help their memories. Researchers have found that it is stimulating to the brain. We might all benefit from wearing a crown of rosemary."

"The herb of remembrance - I like that! I can tell it has already effected *my* memory. I could never forget this invigorating aroma. It is indescribably wonderful! Oh, and now I know where the lamb's ears plants are," he added, pointing enthusiastically to a large mound of soft, gray leaves.

It was almost lunch time when they completed their tour. Faye suggested that they share the picnic lunch in Justin's backpack on the porch. The invitation was quickly accepted and the three sauntered off gaily toward the house. Faye beckoned Pitter and Justin to come in while she tended the plants in her basket. Pitter balked. He had rarely been inside a human's home. The prospect bothered him immensely. But after a bit of pleading and

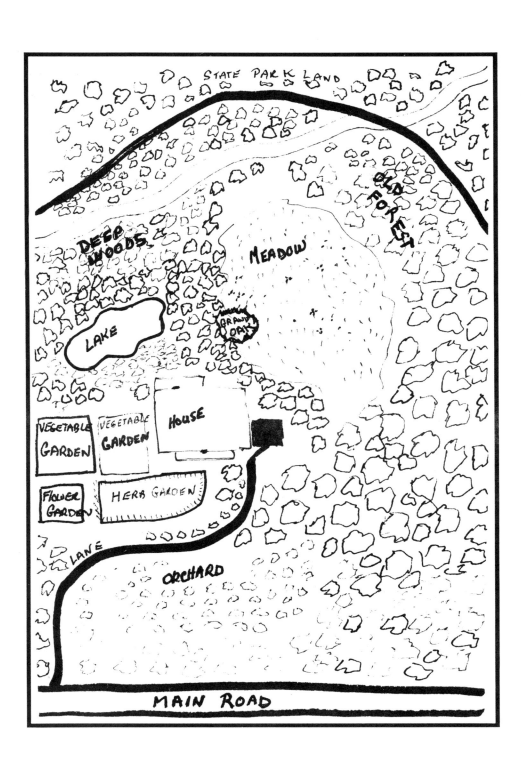

coaxing, he followed Justin and Faye indoors.

At first he flitted around nervously. It was not at all as he had expected. He had heard stories of how untidy human's homes could be -- how cluttered and smelly. This home was different. It was very neat and clean and orderly. Any fairy would be impressed. And above all, it didn't smell. There was a pleasant aroma of fresh baked bread as well as the sweet smells coming from the herbs Faye was hanging in small bunches to dry. Other than that, the air seemed pure, and quite pleasant.

His anxiety faded and his curiosity took over. He fluttered here and there inspecting every nook and cranny. The pictures on the walls caught his attention and he fluttered from one to another asking questions as he went.

"Who are these humans?"

"Justin's father and mother. Justin's mother is my child."

"What about this one?"

"That was Justin as a baby. If you look closely you can see the dimple in his right cheek."

Pitter looked. Then flitted over to peer intently at Justin who couldn't help breaking into an embarrassed grin. Yes, Pitter could see the dimple. Why hadn't he noticed it before, he wondered. Playfully he tickled it with his finger then swept back to the next frame. This one was different. There were no people. It appeared to be a map. He shot a questioning look at Faye.

"Oh, that's a map of our place here. It's supposed to be an aerial view showing where everything is. It's not a very good drawing. I did it myself. See, here's the house where we are now. There's the herb garden where we met this morning. Over here is the old growth forest where Owl lives. This is the State Park land that adjoins my property. Here's the main road." She continued to point out the different areas as Pitter listened and watched attentively. He could see how the map would be very helpful in finding your way around and he was amazed at all of the many natural features contained inside its bounds. This was an uncommon place, with marvelous potential, but it needed the Fairy Touch. He wondered if he should mention this.

The teakettle Justin was tending began to whistle. At first Pitter was quite startled by it, then realized there was nothing to fear. Justin poured the steaming contents into a lovely blue and white teapot. Then he added a scoop of colorful leaves and petals. Justin hovered over the pot inhaling the vapors ascending from its spout. He named them one by one. "Mint and rose and lavender and a touch of something I can't quite place."

"Lemongrass." Faye said.

"Ah, yes." Pitter replied, remembering. "That was the large clump of lemon smelling grass in the corner of the herb garden by the gate."

"Yes." Faye answered, delighted that he had remembered.

"Would you like a cup of tea?" Justin asked. "Grandma has a tiny tea service here in the cupboard with a cup that should be just the right size for you."

Pitter flew over to examine the tea service. The cup fit his hand quite nicely and would hold just the right amount of liquid to quench his thirst. He beamed his approval. Since Pitter was enjoying his exploration of the house, they decided to eat at the kitchen table in front of the large window that overlooked the woods. Soon, the unlikely trio was sipping tea and partaking of the wholesome lunch Faye had provided. Pitter was quite pleased with the tea and proclaimed it a wonderful combination of plant essences. And although he had said the day before that fairies never get hungry like humans, he ate quite heartily in his strange fairy way.

After lunch, he led them back outside. While it was a pleasant enough house, the confines of being indoors was beginning to wear. The afternoon air was unseasonably warm. Only a few puffy white clouds skidded across the sky. They sought the coolness of the woods and savored the shade provided by a thick canopy of leaves. As they meandered about, a soft murmur seemed to follow them. The presence of this fairy boy was creating quite a stir among the plant kingdom. They all wanted to know where he came from and, most of all, was he staying? It had been *so* long since they had seen fairies.

There it was again, Pitter thought. That troubling question. Why are there no fairies in this place? It is perfect for fairies. Better than The Golden Valley where his clan lived. So, why were there none living here? At last he could not suppress the question any longer.

"Faye, I must respectfully ask you something." he began.

Without a moment's hesitation, Faye said, "Ask me anything.

"This is a wondrous place." Pitter began. "It is obvious that all the wild things are happy here. It is *almost* perfect. But, there is something missing. The plant spirits have told me there are no fairies here - haven't been for years and years. Grand Oak said the same thing. I have found no evidence of any myself. Surely there once were. It is obvious they have not been driven out by all the thoughtless means most humans use. I see no sign of harsh chemicals, no sign of burning or building that would disturb them. The water seems pure and the air unusually clean. I can't understand this. Why are there no fairies here? What happened to them?"

Faye stood motionless, her face filled with pain. Tears began to trickle down her cheeks. "It is all my fault," she blurted.

"How can it be your fault, Grandma?" Justin asked. "You have spent your whole life tending this place - protecting it."

"Not my whole life." she answered quietly. "Many years ago when I was a young girl, this place was full of fairies. My mother and father knew this and told me so. I did not believe them. I thought fairies were childish fantasies. I made fun of my parents for believing. One day, my father brought me a fairy tale book. I had wanted a chemistry book instead. I became quite angry with him. I ran outside and stood in the middle of the lane. I started shouting as loud as I could shout, 'I don't believe in fairies! There are no fairies!' I shouted this over and over again. The next day, it was so quiet you could hear a petal fall from a calendula blossom. Not a bird sang, not a frog croaked, not a single wild thing could be heard. The tree branches drooped, not a leaf moved, not a breeze stirred. The plants wilted and all the flowers shriveled and fell off. It was a ghastly thing. That was the day Grand Oak first made himself known to me. He told me the fairies had all left in the night. They could not bear to live where they were not wanted. He said I had done an evil, hateful thing. Too late, I had learned to believe. Ever since then, I have tried to make amends. But the fairies have never returned."

Pitter listened carefully. So that explained it. Of course, no fairy clan would stay where a child did not believe. What a dreadful time it must have been for that family of fairies. His heart went out to them. But that was long ago. It was obvious Faye had learned her lesson well and he was touched by the depth of her remorse and all she had done since in restitution.

"I am saddened to learn what happened to the fairy clan that once dwelled here," Pitter said finally. "But I accept that you are sincerely sorry. It was a childish transgression - one that happens all too frequently. Few children believe in fairies these days. And those who do believe, think they all lived across The Great Sea and disappeared many years ago. What foolishness that is! Have you lived here ever since?"

"No," Faye answered. "When I grew up, I could not bear to be here, knowing what I had done. I went away to school, got married, and raised a family away from here. I came back only for visits. My parents spent the rest of their lives nurturing this place, trying to coax the fairies back. When they died, they left it all to me. My husband and I moved here to carry on their work. I really owe all of this to them. But even after all these years, not a single fairy has thought to make this their home.

Pitter understood why. There was no doubt that in their quest to set things right, they had created and preserved the ideal environment for fairies. The problem now was gaining trust. Any traveling fairies who came upon this place would view it with suspicion. Uppermost in their minds would be the question, 'if this place is so perfect, why aren't there fairies already here?' Finding no answer, they would decide there must be troubles afoot that they cannot discern, and move quickly on. While he was absorbed with that thought, another question popped into his mind.

"How is it that you are sighted now?"

"I have traveled through many countries learning all I can about fairies. Some years ago, in Ireland, I chanced upon a special charm that was said to invoke the presence of a fairy. It worked. A charming fairy lady appeared. We spent a lovely afternoon together. Before she left, she gave me Fairy Sight. Of course, since there have been no fairies here, I've had no chance to use it - until now."

"I wish I could help." Pitter said. "I know this to be a fine place and you, to have fine intentions. If I could, I would direct Travelers who come to The Golden Valley to come here to live. But, I only journey here when I sleep-fly and do not know the way. Perhaps, some day when I have all my powers, I will know how to find this place when I am awake. Then I will send fairies who need a home, to live here."

The underlying message in what Pitter had just said had a profound effect on Justin and Faye. They had so hoped Pitter would decide to stay, but it was apparent that he was going back. He looked at their stunned, disappointed faces and realized they already knew what he was about to tell them.

"I must return home tonight." he said, confirming their fears. "My mother is surely frantic with worry and I have responsibilities to my clan. Perhaps, I will return again from time-to-time, since my sleep-flying episodes always bring me here. I wish I could stay, but I can't."

"We understand." Faye said. "Family must always come first. We will miss you."

"When will you leave?" asked Justin.

"After the darkness comes. I'm hoping that if I fall asleep focusing all my powers on returning home, I will sleep-fly there. It is my only hope."

The three friends spent the rest of the afternoon exploring the woods. Faye and Justin showed Pitter where they had planted the goldenseal and ginseng rootlets. Pitter flitted to and fro over the colonies of fledging plants. All the while, he hummed a strange tune and sprinkled a fine dust from his wand. It sparkled and glistened on each plant for a brief second, then magically disappeared.

When evening came, they said their farewells and Pitter flew off toward the Old Forest. Justin and Faye stood frozen in place watching long after he had gone. Reluctantly and with heavy hearts, they finally headed home.

Chapter Six

Darkness found Pitter lying on his pillow high up in a syca-more tree. He squeezed his eyes shut and focused on The Golden Valley. Minutes passed. Hours passed. Try as he might, he could not make himself go to sleep. Maybe, he was trying *too* hard. He got up and stretched. The tree he had chosen was high on a hill-side above the Old Forest. The view from where he was standing was magnificent. He could see for miles and miles. Below was Jus-tin and Faye's home. It was dark there. They would have gone to sleep hours ago. He stared out across the wide expanse of sky. The moon cast a bright, soft glow over the land. The stars twinkled. This would be an exceptional night for dancing in The Golden Val-ley. He could just envision the other fairies dressed in their best frocks and tunics, pirouetting round and round on a carpet of fairy moss. Maybe, if he tried again, he could make himself sleep-fly back to where he truly belonged. He turned to retrieve his pillow and look for a more comfortable spot.

Just then, a flash of white light captured his attention. He wheeled around just in time to see a shooting star plummet swiftly toward earth. He stiffened. This could only mean one thing. Instantly, his wand was in his hand. He placed the star-shaped end against his chest and waited. The shooting star vanished. In its wake, a shimmering silver trail reached back into the heavens - a trail only visible to fairies and angels.

Pitter watched intently, knowing what was about to follow,

wondering whose time it was. A small multicolored globe of light began to ascend the glittering pathway. Up and up it went, rising smoothly and swiftly, higher and higher. Pitter poured all of his focus toward the light. He wanted desperately to know who the fairy was, making the journey to the Other Realm. All at once, he felt a strange quiver run through him. Only a King's aura was multicolored. Trembling, he focused harder. A wave of awareness spread over him that was unmistakable. Grandfather! It was Grandfather who was passing into the Other Realm. Shaking with disbelief, and then sadness, he raised his wand in reverent salute. The light was now high up in the heavens - just a small dot against the vast expanse of space, marking the spot of his grandfather's entry into the Other Realm. The pathway quickly faded and was gone. It had all taken only three human seconds.

Pitter stood silently watching the new star for a long time. With a mixture of emotions, he realized it was next to his father's. He could not bear to look another moment, to be in their presence. Grabbing his pillow, he flew down to the forest floor in a daze. Stumbling about, his body quaking with grief, he found a hollow log and crawled inside. He did not want anyone to see him or hear him, not even the forest creatures. He curled himself into a small ball and cried, and cried, and cried. Sometime later, he was aware that it was raining. The Earth was crying too.

It rained for three days and three nights. A soft, gray, sorrowful looking rain. Justin watched it from his window. Even his grandmother commented on what a strange look it had to it. It was like a pall of sadness had fallen over the woods and forest and the meadow. They spent their time taking care of indoor chores and playing games. They planned a few additions to the herb and vegetable gardens. And Faye worked on a new children's book she was writing. Occasionally, she would ask Justin for his help with it. Through those long rainy hours, their thoughts turned frequently to Pitter. They missed him but were happy to think of him at home in his Golden Valley, safely among his own kind. And he had promised to send fairies their way at the first opportunity. The prospect filled them with excitement.

They were relieved when the rain finally stopped late in the evening on the third day. It was beginning to fill them with a strange sense of melancholy. When morning came, the sun greeted them. The clouds were gone and everything was bathed in warmth and light. It was a startling and welcome contrast to the previous days' gloom.

Justin and his grandmother set to work, catching up on outdoor chores. The day passed quickly. When evening came, the two were quite exhausted but filled with satisfaction at all they had accomplished. The weather report on the television predicted another fine day tomorrow. Tired and content, Justin went off to bed.

In the middle of the night, he was awakened by a strange noise. Startled, he sat up and looked around. A small speck of faint purple light hovered outside his window bumping against the screen over and over, as if trying to get in. Pitter? Justin scurried over and pushed the screen up. The small winged object fluttered in, wobbling from side to side as if injured. It came to rest on the note pad on his desk. Justin could tell in the dim light that it must be a fairy. A very dirty fairy. One that smelled of mold and mildew and was covered in mud except for one small spot where a dim purple glimmer shown through.

"Pitter? Is that you, Pitter?" Justin asked. He could not quite believe this could really be his fairy friend, but who else could it be?

"Yes." came a weak reply. "May I sleep here with you? I must get some rest and I cannot bear to be alone any longer. I'm so cold and tired. So very, very tired."

Justin's mind was in a turmoil. Whatever had happened to Pitter? It was obvious that he had had a very bad time. He was anxious to press him for more information, but knew his friend was beyond answering. He had fallen fast asleep on the note pad. Justin gently picked him up. He weighs no more than a hummingbird, Justin thought, remembering the exquisitely iridescent bird that had flown into the window last summer. It had been killed instantly and Justin had buried it under the bee balm, which seemed to be its favorite. It had weighed no more than a cotton ball. Pitter felt the same. Justin carefully placed him on a soft pillow on the chair. He covered him with a folded handkerchief and then went back to bed. Later, he was again awakened by muffled sobs. He got up to check on Pitter and found him still laying where he had left him - still fast asleep. But he was crying. Justin stayed awake the rest of the night watching over him.

When morning came, he tiptoed out of his room, leaving Pitter still resting soundly on the chair. The sun was just beginning to rise but his grandmother was already in the kitchen brewing tea. She was quite surprised to see Justin up so early.

"Come with me, Grandma. Pitter is back." Justin urged, taking her hand.

Puzzled she followed him into his room. She quickly covered her mouth to stifle a gasp of surprise.

"Are you sure that's Pitter? This poor creature is so dirty. How can you tell?" she whispered.

"He told me, right before he went to sleep," Justin said.

"But look at him. He's so dirty and smelly. What in heaven's name happened to this dear boy? We must help him clean himself up when he awakens. I'll get things ready."

66

She hurried off. Justin remained keeping vigil over his friend, all the while wondering what terrible circumstances had brought him to this state. It was the middle of the afternoon when Pitter finally awoke. At first he seemed to have no recollection of where he was or what had happened to him. He was surprised to find himself on a pillow in a house. Slowly he began to remember the events of the last few days. Grief overwhelmed him again but this time, he was all cried out. He looked down at himself and couldn't believe his eyes. His nose wrinkled up in disgust. He started to get up and fell over. His legs felt so weak and his head was spinning.

"You need to go slowly." Justin said. He had been watching from the end of his bed, conscious that Pitter was unaware of his presence.

Pitter looked at him and Justin immediately saw the lively gleam in his eyes was gone. They were dull and listless. Pitter tried to stand again and lost his balance. Justin caught him.

"Maybe, if I stand you on my desk, it will help." he suggested. "That pillow would be difficult for anyone to stand on."

He carefully set Pitter down on the desk and slowly let go.

"Yes. This is better." Pitter agreed.

He took a few tentative steps, then tried to move his wings. They were so caked in dirt, they would not budge. Just then, Faye entered the room carrying a tray.

"So, you're awake at last." she said cheerfully. "I've brought some things to help clean you up. You must feel dreadful with all that mud on you and you're in no condition to take care of this by yourself. I brought bowls of soapwort solution to wash you and your clothes in, a cup of lavender water to rinse with, and some horsetail to polish your wings. These should do the trick."

"Yes." Pitter said passively. "They are just the right things. But I fear I'm too weak to care."

"You'll feel much better after you've had a bath." Faye insisted. "But first I would like you to drink this."

"What is it?" he asked as he took the tiny teacup from her.

"A drop of a famous Bach flower remedy. Many believe it is very helpful for anyone who has suffered a terrible loss or shock, which must be the case with you."

Pitter did not comment, but sipped the drop of liquid obediently and handed the cup back to Faye. "Perhaps, this *will* help. I have heard of Edmund Bach and his flower remedies from Travelers who came across The Great Sea. They said he was an exceptional human with an extraordinary level of discernment, not unlike our own. They revered him."

"I'm not surprised." Faye answered. "Now, let's see what we can do about getting you clean."

Justin helped Pitter out of his tunic and into the bowl of soapwort. He handed him a tiny cloth. Little by little, with much effort and encouragement, he washed himself. In the meantime, Faye dunked his tunic into another bowl of soapwort and scrubbed it clean. When Pitter was finished bathing, Justin poured the lavender water over him gently. Then they gave him a small towel to pat himself dry, and another one to wrap himself in while his clothes dried. Faye cut two slits in the back of the towel for his wings to fit through. Realizing he must be hungry, Justin carried him out to the kitchen. They brewed a pot of herbal tea and set some bread and fresh fruit in front of him. The effort of eating soon exhausted him and it wasn't long before he dozed off again. It was a curious sight - a tiny fairy boy wrapped in a towel, asleep on the kitchen table.

When he awoke, his clothes were dry, and with Justin's help, he dressed himself. Then Faye took some of the horsetail and polished his wings. When she was finished, he looked like the Pitter they had known before - almost. The mischievous gleam in his eyes was still missing, and the purple glow he usually emitted was only half as bright as it used to be. He was noticeably better than he had been when he first arrived, but a long way from recovery.

"You must tell us what has happened to you, Pitter." Faye said.

They listened with great concern and sympathy as the story of the last few days unfolded. Pitter told them of his grandfather, his role as future King, the encounter in The Golden Valley, the Circles of Attunement, and his grandfather's disappointment in him. He decided not to tell them the story of Betwixt Between. He now knew the grave significance of those two words, and did not want to share them with humans - even these two.

But he did tell them about seeing his grandfather pass to the Other Realm. Although they had never heard of such a thing before, they knew it must be so, if Pitter said it was. Finally, he told them of the days and nights he spent in the log, unable to control his grief. And how, after the rain stopped, he had found himself lying in a mud puddle inside the decaying tree. He had felt so stiff and feeble. It had taken him several human hours to make it to the house and Justin's window.

"So," Pitter continued. "I cannot go back now, even though I want to. I know everyone must blame me for Grandfather's death. I blame myself. He was old and frail and close to the end of his earthly assignment. I should have known better. The stress I caused him must have been more than he could bear. Now I have no choice but to stay here. To return, would only cause everyone more pain. I'm sure I am no longer welcome there."

They had wanted him to stay, but not this way. Their hearts went out to him.

"I wish I could hug you." Faye said. "But you are too small and I am too big."

"Yes, it is true." Pitter agreed. "I would very much like to have a hug. It is what I miss the most. But I have brought this on myself and have no one else to blame. It will be my punishment for turning my back on the people who loved me - for not appreciating what I had. I must somehow learn to live without hugs."

They sat quietly together for a long time. There was little else to say. Only time could soften the ache in Pitter's heart. Toward evening, Pitter seemed to have regained much of his strength. He flew to the window and looked out longingly toward the Old Forest.

"I think I would like to spend the night in Owl's tree." he said at last. "I must get used to being alone."

They watched him go, knowing he would be back tomorrow. He needed them now, as he had not before.

Chapter Seven

The next morning, Justin and Faye were already hard at work in the herb garden when Pitter arrived. They were surprised and delighted that his cheery disposition had returned. The anguish of the day before seemed to have disappeared. They knew better, but accepted his courageous attempt to put his grief and troubles behind him. He quickly made himself a rosemary crown and plopped it on his head with a flourish. Then, he slipped on the lamb's ears wing covers Faye had waiting for him.

"I have very much appreciated your thoughtfulness in making these for me, Faye." he said. "But now that I am staying, I must do this for myself. Perhaps, if I expose my wings to a little sun each day, they will become conditioned to it. There is much to learn about being a day fairy. And I want to help with everything."

"What would you like to do?" Justin asked.

"Well, this is truly a fine place, but it definitely could use the Fairy Touch. Plant spirits respond much better to fairies than to humans. No offense! It is just the way of nature. See those sickly marjoram plants over there? I noticed them the first day. They're miserable. You know why? Because they feel smothered by those tall basils towering over them. They can hardly breathe. I asked them to tell me what would make them feel better and they were quick to say they'd like to be over in that open space by the thyme."

Faye looked at the marjoram, then at the space Pitter indicated. Yes, it made perfect sense. Why hadn't she thought of this.

71

Without a moment's hesitation, she took the trowel and began to lift the plants from the soil. Remembering the plant spirit's feelings, she made sure to explain what she was doing and why before she began. When they were in place in their new surroundings, she made a shelter over them to protect them from the hot sun.

"That's very good." Pitter said, approvingly. "Transplanting is such a terrible shock. It's always wise to provide the plants with some protection for a day or two while they settle in. But what do we have here?" He stopped to gaze at a cluster of small nasturtium plants that seemed to be struggling. He raised a leaf and peeked at its underside. Sure enough - aphids! Lots and lots of aphids. He checked others. Same thing. "Never fear, little plants," he said reassuringly. "I have just the solution."

He flew off to the other side of the garden and was back in a jiffy. In each hand he carried a ladybug. He placed them on a nasturtium leaf and headed off to get more. Justin and Faye helped. Before long, an army of speckled ladybugs was voraciously chomping its way through a feast of aphids. "It's all part of the Great Master Plan," Pitter said. "If humans had a better understanding of maintaining balance, they could eliminate almost all of those dreadful chemicals they use. You have done well, Faye, to encourage a wonderful supply of beneficial insects. No wonder there are few problems in your garden."

Having handled the aphid situation, they strolled further down the garden path pinching back gangly basils and mints. Pitter's gaze wandered taking in other areas of the garden. His eyes came to rest on an area close to the fence. "See the sage plant over there, Faye?" he said, pointing. "I can't help noticing most of it is woody and spent. The only real life is right at the ends. This is an old grandfather plant. He is very weary of being kept alive and wants to pass on. His only reason for staying now is to provide nourishment for the grandchildren on the end of the stems. He must be allowed to complete his cycle with dignity."

"I could take cuttings from the ends and root them." Faye said. "Then we could dig up what is left and add it to the compost pile. That way he could live on in the new plants his grandchildren create and in the soil he nourishes later."

"Exactly - a dignified passage. It's what we all want!" Pitter cried. "And wait until I tell you what the hyssop told me."

They spent all morning and most of the afternoon, tending the herb garden. Pitter flitted from plant to plant, communing with the plant spirits and finding out the state of their health. Most were doing quite nicely and had very kind things to say about the care Faye and Justin had been giving them. Only a few needed some extra attention. But as happy as they were with the excellent care they had been receiving, they all agreed it was quite wonderful to have a fairy looking after them too. It brought a sense of enchantment to the garden they had sorely missed.

Late in the afternoon, the three companions went for a walk in the peaceful woods behind the house to check on the ginseng and goldenseal. Justin and Faye could not believe their eyes. The tiny plants were ten times larger than they had been when Pitter sprinkled them with fairy dust. They were sturdier and healthier and it appeared that every single one was growing.

"You are right, Pitter." Faye told him. "This place really needed the Fairy Touch."

"I've been thinking." Pitter mused. "We are constantly referring to 'this place'. It should have a real name. Fairies always give the place they live a name. I have been told that when my clan finally found where they now live, it was what humans call autumn. As far as the eye could see, there were trees bedecked in brilliant yellows and golds. It was a crisp, clear day and the sun was shining so brightly that the whole valley seemed to be encased in gold.

That's why they named it The Golden Valley."

"I've thought about this before." Faye said. "But I've never been able to come up with a name I liked or one that seemed to fit."

"I have." Pitter replied smugly, then continued. "I think from now on it should be called The Land of Faye. For two reasons: First, Faye is your name and you are responsible for this place being what it is today. Second, in some places, as I told you before, fairies have been called fays, and fays are exactly what you have been fervently hoping would come to live here. It's perfect. I'm quite proud of myself for thinking of it!"

"Yes." Justin agreed wholeheartedly. "It *is* perfect. The Land of Faye. That's what we should call it from now on."

Pitter was delighted. As if to make it official, he raised his arms up in the air and yelled as loud as he could, "Beginning today, this is The Land of Faye." Then he caught himself and began to chuckle. "Hey, that rhymes, doesn't it? Did I tell you I love rhymes?"

"I think so." Justin said politely. "But it has been a long time since I heard you make one." The look of satisfaction on Pitter's face warmed their hearts.

Feeling slightly embarrassed by Pitter's proclamation, Faye smiled and said, "Thank you, Pitter. Suggesting such a thing makes me realize you truly do forgive me for driving the fairies away all those years ago. And you are here with us now. There really is hope for The Land of Faye."

Chapter Eight

Bustling spring days gave way to long, lazy, summer ones filled with picnics in the woods, hikes through the Old Forest, romps in the meadow. The herb garden flourished under Pitter's watchful eye, as did the woodlands. Every morning, he began the day by making himself a rosemary crown and lamb's ears wing covers. As the weeks wore on, his wings became less sensitive to the sun and required the extra protection only now and then on the brightest days. He was convinced that the rosemary had helped adjust his sleep patterns from day to night - so much so, that he had become quite partial to being a day fairy.

One early summer afternoon, found Justin and Pitter lounging near the lake in the woods. Pitter had just ridden the bullfrog for the umpteenth time and was dripping wet. Sprawled on a bed of moss, he waited for the warm breezes to dry him off. Near the edge of the lake, not far from them, a mother duck sat on her nest of eggs in a clump of reeds. It would not be long before her ducklings hatched. Pitter and Justin had been keeping a close watch on her, and them, for days.

"I wonder what it would be like to ride a duck." Pitter said.

Overhearing this, the mother duck turned her head and stared at him incredulously with her dark, glassy eye.

"Don't you *even* think about it!" she retorted.

Pitter laughed. "Don't worry, Mother Duck. You have your hands full, and will for some time. I'll just be content with my rides on that accommodating green gentleman snoozing on the lily pad."

"If only I could ride the bullfrog too." Justin said wistfully.

"I know." Pitter said. "I feel badly that I can't help."

"Do you think you will ever get all of your powers?" Justin asked.

"Maybe." Pitter replied. "I noticed just this morning that another one of the circles on my hand has disappeared. I don't know when it happened. It always puzzles me. There are only three left now. Perhaps, if I am ever able to rid myself of all of them, my powers will come to me. I feel like only half a fairy without them."

"It must be quite wonderful to be a fairy, especially if you have all your powers." Justin ventured. "But there are many things I don't understand about fairies."

"Like what?" Pitter asked.

"Well, in the fairy tales I've read, all the fairies are in England or Wales, or Ireland, or Greece. How did fairies get to America?"

"Silly!" Pitter laughed. "It is a misconception that all fairies lived only on the other side of The Great Sea. It is likewise wrong to believe that if there are fairies here, they must have come from over there. Perhaps, it was the other way around. The currents of The Great Sea flow both ways. Fairies have always been here. Before the First People came, there were fairies. "

"The First People?"

"You call them Native Americans. Some people incorrectly call them Indians."

"Oh!. Fairies were here before they were?"

"Yes. They never would have survived without us. We taught them which plants to use for food and medicine. They were our friends. We lived in harmony with them for thousands of human years. Things were very different then. In those days, our squirrel friends would tell of traveling all the way from the Mighty

Dividing River to The Great Sea in the east, without ever leaving the tree tops."

"The Mighty Dividing River?" Justin interrupted.

"Yes. They call it the Mississippi now. But not then, when the land was unspoiled. It was not until after the New Ones came that things changed. They brought sickness we could not fight. They brought ideas we could not live with. They drove the First People away. They drove us into hiding."

"Wow!" Justin exclaimed. "That's terrible."

"Yes. More terrible that you can ever imagine. Take for instance the ginseng plants you and your grandmother planted? Back then, no one would ever have believed it would one day be endangered. Ginseng plants were everywhere, with roots so big and so abundant that children made dolls from them to play with."

"What happened?"

"The First People shared our secrets of the ginseng with the New Ones. They thought they would respect the Earth and the plants as they did. They were wrong. Soon the woodlands were overrun with people digging up all the precious roots. Not just ginseng, but goldenseal, bloodroot, wild ginger and others. Most of these were loaded onto large ships and sent back across The Great Sea. Little by little, the plants disappeared. Only those hidden in very remote places survived - but not for long. Sadly, the demand is even greater today than it was then. Almost every hiding place has been found, and the plants taken. There are hardly any left in the wild places. If it weren't for people like you and your grandmother, they would be very close to extinction - just like the passenger pigeon my people loved and lost to the New Ones."

"Gee! Grandma and I should do even more. Maybe, if I save my allowance and do chores for extra money, I could buy a lot more rootlets to plant in the woods."

"That's a very good idea. And since this is my home now, I'll certainly do my part to help them grow. I've been thinking. There should also be a fine crop of seeds in the Old Forest this year. I plan to look after them and make sure they have a chance to sprout. But we must not tell others. They will come in the dark of night and steal them. This has happened many times in The Golden Valley. There are none left there now."

Just then, a loud commotion interrupted them. So engrossed were they in their conversation, they had not noticed a large snake slithering across the grass toward the duck's nest of eggs. She had just stood up to fluff her feathers when she spotted him. Instantly she darted at him squawking and clucking. Just as quickly, the drake came charging from his napping place in the bushes. But the snake was too large and too intent on his prey to be thwarted by those outraged parents. Pitter and Justin jumped up just as the snake made a lunge at the nest. Without a second to waste, Pitter reacted immediately. A brilliant flash from his wand zapped the snake in the head and sent him writhing into a wriggly coil.

"That will teach you!" Pitter said sternly. He was happy to see that at least of few of his powers worked. "I know you have to eat," he chastised. "But why take advantage of ducklings who haven't even had a chance at life? Go work for your dinner and don't let this ever happen again. While you're at it, tell the rest of the snake kingdom, these eggs are off limits." Shamed by the fairy boy's criticism, the snake made a hasty retreat.

Still shaking from the upset, Mother Duck and her husband, the Drake, deluged Pitter with thank you's as the snake sulked off.

"You saved our babies." they cried. "We owe their lives to you. If we can ever do anything for you, no matter what, just ask."

Pitter looked at Mother Duck with a grin and then mischievously raised an eyebrow. *"Anything?"* he asked.

"Yes, you fairy rascal!" she clucked. "I'll *even* take you for a ride after my babies are hatched. It's the least I can do!"

Pitter clapped his hands with glee, spun around twice and leaped in the air tapping his heels together. He could hardly wait.

The excitement behind them, Justin and Pitter went back to lounging in the shade and resumed their conversation.

"The Land of Faye continues to pose questions for me." Pitter said, as he stretched out on his favorite spot of moss.

"What kinds of questions?" Justin asked.

"Well, I really shouldn't pry, but it puzzles me. I know humans have a great dependence on the coins and paper bills you call money. How do you get the money to provide the things here that you need?"

"My grandmother inherited money when her parents died, and again when my grandfather died. Besides, she gets paid a lot for books she writes and classes she gives during the winter. That's when she does most of her traveling. She never likes to be away from here in the spring and summer."

"Ah! I can understand why."

"Now I have a question," Justin said. "How do you know about money if you have avoided humans for years and years?"

"You are a quick one!" Pitter laughed. "We learn these things by various means. Travelers from other lands tell us. Fairies who have lived near cities tell us. There are many ways. Most, I cannot tell you. Some things must remain, in the fairy domain! Hey, I made a rhyme! I love rhymes. I guess I told you that."

"Yes, I believe you did."

Justin and Pitter spent the rest of the afternoon telling stories and playing games. as the bond of friendship between them deepened. It was a magical summer day, surpassing anything either had ever experienced.

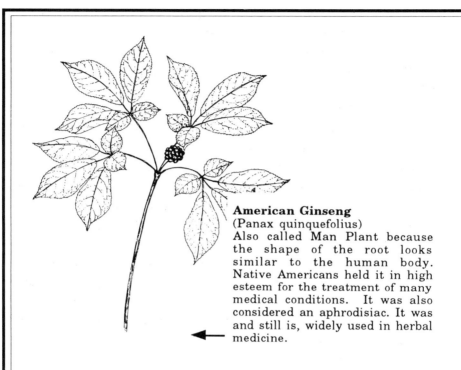

American Ginseng
(Panax quinquefolius)
Also called Man Plant because the shape of the root looks similar to the human body. Native Americans held it in high esteem for the treatment of many medical conditions. It was also considered an aphrodisiac. It was and still is, widely used in herbal medicine.

Goldenseal
(Hydrastis canadensis)
Also called Indian Paint and Wild Turmeric. As these names imply, it has been used as a dye plant. Goldenseal has a long history in traditional herbal medicine that continues today.

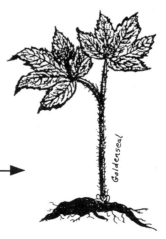

Chapter Nine

In The Golden Valley, there were more pressing matters to deal with. Since the King's passing, the fairy clan had been in chaos. The King had never regained consciousness after his accident and so the decision regarding who should be King, was left to his Prime Minister. This was quite a dilemma. Always the first born had assumed the royal crown. But Pitter was gone. Some had been overheard to cattily say, 'good riddance'.

For several weeks, the Prime Minister struggled with this crucial decision as the affairs of the kingdom went unaddressed. In the end, there seemed to be no other choice but to make Patter the King. Patter objected strenuously pointing out his lack of leadership skills, his inability to make decisions, his penchant for wanting to please everyone all the time. A King must be able to lead and make decisions even though some might disagree with them, or be displeased. How could Patter ever do that? He pleaded for them to choose another, but in the end, there *was* no one else.

Patter finally had no other alternative but to assume the crown. With a heart filled with fear and foreboding, he reluctantly began his reign. By that time, the state of the kingdom was in disarray. Patter was overwhelmed with all the many problems there were to deal with. No longer could he join the others in dances in the moonlight. There was nothing but work, work, work. If only Pitter would come back. Pitter could handle all of this and still find time for dancing. Patter was sure of that. It was the only thing he was sure of.

Considering his state of mind, it is no wonder that when the outer guards sent what should have been a disturbing message to the Fairy Council, he brushed it aside. It seems they had observed a number of human families loading large trucks with all of their belongings and moving out of the valley. On one hand, this might be welcome news. Fairies always believed the fewer humans, the better. But there was something ominous, even sinister, about this. The outer guards were deeply troubled and felt it warranted some investigation.

Patter skimmed over their message and decided any action on his part could surely wait. With the humans gone, maybe their water would be cleaner, their air more pleasant to breathe. He saw no cause for worry. Instead, he decided their leaving was probably a good thing. Quickly, he dismissed the whole affair and placed the message on the bottom of his pile of things to think about - later. Arrogantly, he congratulated himself. Perhaps, he had sold himself short. He could do this job after all - maybe even better than Pitter.

Chapter Ten

Summer days in The Land of Faye were glorious beyond words. The flowers and the herbs were bursting with bloom. The vegetable garden was laden with all sorts of colorful, nutritious things to eat. And the trees and bushes in the orchard drooped with lush fruits and berries. Faye and Justin spent many long hours harvesting and preserving all this wonderful bounty.

Fragrant herbs were hung to dry on beams in the kitchen. The shelves in the large pantry in the basement groaned from the weight of countless canning jars filled with delectable things. And to think, it was only the middle of August! There was still so much more to come.

Pitter was fascinated by all of this preparation for winter but it troubled him too. He couldn't help but wonder about his own circumstances. Fairies spend the winter underground. It is their duty to tend the roots of the dormant plants and help them weather the coldest season of the year. Granted no one had done that here in The Land of Faye for years. But this was his home now. He must assume this responsibility.

Still, he dreaded the whole idea. Months underground! All alone! The thought sent a shiver through him followed by a deep sense of loss. Always he had looked forward to winter. It was a time of rest and storytelling. Every year, he and Patter would have a contest to see who could find the most nuts the squirrels had buried on the mound. Pitter always won. He smiled to himself thinking how delicious the nuts tasted and how much fun he and Patter had collecting them. But that was then. This is now! No sense dwelling on the past. Tomorrow, Pitter decided, he must go scouting for a fairy mound. He too, must get ready for winter - a long winter alone.

"Over here, Pitter!" Justin cried. "Just look at all of these lovely little white forget-me-nots. They shouldn't be blooming now. Their blossoms are always gone by now."

Pitter swooped past Justin and stopped short, hovering. Carefully he surveyed the small patch of flowers. Strange for them to be in full bloom now. Then it hit him.

"No wonder! They're growing on a fairy mound!" he exclaimed delightedly.

"A fairy mound?"

"Yes. I've been looking for one."

"You've been looking for one?"

"Yes. Now if I can just find the door." he replied, as he flitted to and fro, skimming the surface of a raised area of ground.

"The door?"

"Of course. Fairies used to live here. There has to be a door! "Ah! Here it is." he said triumphantly. "Right next to these pretty forget-me-nots. That's very interesting. They must be blooming to mark the spot, hoping fairies will come to live here again. If you'll excuse me, Justin, I have to check it out inside."

"Inside?"

"Yes! I'm beginning to think there's an echo here!" he said. "You repeat everything I say."

"Sorry." Justin said with a giggle as he watched Pitter disappear through a small cluster of rocks next to the flowers.

Justin waited. After a while he decided to sit down and

picked a spot next to a large colony of butterflyweed. The bright orange blossoms were thick with butterflies and bees sipping their afternoon nectar. All at once, Justin felt a vibration in the ground. Then the plant closest to him started to shake back and forth. Startled, he stood up and looked at the plant intently. He was sure he heard it - giggle! No, that couldn't be. Yes, there it was again. The plant was definitely shaking and giggling. You would think someone was tickling it. A knowing smile spread over his face. Pitter! This had to be Pitter's work.

Just then a small object flashed past his ear. He knew without even looking that it was Pitter.

"How did you do that?" Justin asked.

"Do what?"

"Make this poor plant shake and giggle."

"Ah. I just wanted to give you a little tickle, so I gave its roots a little tickle while I was underground. Worked, didn't it?"

"Yes! You certainly have unusual ways to have fun."

"At least now anyway. I'm not so sure about this winter."

"Why?"

"Fairies must spend the winter underground - in a fairy mound such as this. We have a duty to tend the roots. This mound will make a suitable winter home, but it will be very lonely in there all by myself."

Justin thought about this and had to agree. If only other fairies would find The Land of Faye before winter came. He couldn't imagine spending the winter all alone underground - even with the roots for company.

On their way back to the lake for Pitter's afternoon bullfrog ride, they stopped for a while to talk to Grand Oak.

"So what have you boys been up to?" he boomed.

"Just exploring, Grand Oak." Pitter answered. "In fact, we

found a fairy mound where I can stay this winter."

"Would think you'd get mighty lonely - *mighty* lonely!"

"Yes, that's what I'm afraid of."

The old oak hesitated, then scratched his head with a branch. He seemed to be wrestling with his thoughts, weighing his words. At last he said, "You boys ought to take a walk back in the Deep Woods. I hear there are some lovely, most *unusual* things to see there these days, especially near that old willow tree that hangs over the stream."

Pitter and Justin exchanged puzzled glances. It was obvious Grand Oak had some ulterior motive for wanting them to go there. And, of course, he knew that once their curiosity was aroused, they would not rest until it was satisfied. What were they waiting for? The old oak chuckled as the two scurried off. This should be interesting, he thought. Very interesting!

It was cool and quiet in the Deep Woods. The two kept getting sidetracked as they stopped to admire stands of fairy mushrooms and colonies of fairy smoke. Pitter couldn't help saying one of his rhymes over and over. "Fairy smoke, is no joke! Fairy smoke, is no joke! I love rhymes! But you know that, don't you?" he said, casting a sly look at Justin.

"Yes. You've told me before."

"Do you remember what I told you about the Fairy Smoke?"

"Yes! That they must have called it that because it can disappear into a black ooze so quickly. Now you see it, now you don't! Just like you sometimes! One second you're here and the next, you've vanished. Just like smoke. I should call you Smoke."

"I don't think so!"

"Oops, what was that?"

"What was what?"

"Over there by the willow. I saw a flash of blue light."

"Are you sure?"

"Well, I think - - yes, there it is again!"

"I saw it! My, oh my, oh my, oh my!" Pitter repeated over and over, his eyes fixed on the willow tree in an unbelieving stare. "It's a fairy girl!" he cried.

"You're kidding." Justin answered.

"No, I'm not. I wouldn't kid about anything this big! You in the willow," he called. "Come out and introduce yourself."

They waited. The only sounds they could hear came from skittering chipmunks and singing birds.

"You must be mistaken." Justin said.

"No! I'm not. I know a fairy when I see one. And I saw this one. Just for a split second, but long enough. She's here all right."

"We're perfectly harmless," he called again. "Come out so we can meet you. My name is Pitter. This is my friend, Justin. He may be human, but he won't hurt you. I give you my word."

Again they waited, all of their attention focused on the tree where they had last seen the blue light.

"So what are *you* doing here fairy boy?" a very bold, female voice asked sarcastically from somewhere behind them.

Startled, they wheeled around. There she was, perched on a bush several feet away. Arms crossed in front of her, head cocked to one side, she glared at them in a most aggressive way. Justin was worried. Pitter was enormously annoyed.

"I told you my name is Pitter - not 'fairy boy'." he shot back.

Ignoring this, she said, "I thought this place was deserted. I thought no other fairies lived here!"

"Well, I do! Pitter retorted. "And 'this place' has a name, just as I do. It's called The Land of Faye. What's your name and where did you come from?"

"My name is Alaina and that's all you need to know," she

responded. Her overbearing attitude perturbed Pitter immensely.

The fairy girl stared at Pitter long and hard. He stared back. Neither blinked or moved. Justin watched intrigued. Who would ever have thought he would witness a stare-down between two fairies? Neither flinched. They just stared and stared until Justin thought their eyes would surely pop out of their heads. The air around them felt electrified. This was incredible.

Unexpectedly, at exactly the same instant, they both broke into a broad, beguiling smile like nothing Justin had ever seen before. Eyes still locked, they started to giggle. Before long, they were laughing outloud. Then, just as abruptly as it had begun, the laughter stopped and they stared deeply and solemnly into each other's eyes. All the while, that same curious smile played around the corners of their mouths. Then, for no reason Justin could see, Pitter started turning cartwheels on the soft grass.

"He loves me!" Alaina declared matter-of-factly to Justin.

"How do you know?" Justin asked in a state of shock.

"He just fell head over heels in front of me."

"Well, she loves me too." Pitter shouted with a happiness in his voice that astounded Justin.

"How do *you* know?" he asked, totally baffled by all of this.

"She's blushing - look! The only time a fairy girl blushes is when she first feels true love."

"Wow!" Justin marveled. "Now what?"

"Watch closely." Pitter ordered, giving him a wink.

All at once, there was an enormous, blinding flash of light and before him stood Pitter and Alaina dressed in what had to be wedding clothes. There was no mistaking it. Justin stared in stunned silence. Pitter wore a tunic that seemed to be spun of fine golden threads. The neck and sleeves and hem were trimmed in bands of silver. On his head, was a crown woven of rosemary, accented with gilded roses. And from head to toe, he was wrapped

in a dazzling radiance. And then there was Alaina - a vision so lovely, it took his breath away. She was dressed in a gown of spun gold
sprinkled with tiny, shimmering diamonds. And if that weren't
enough, she wore a necklace and a tiara of diamonds, emeralds and
pearls. Like Pitter, she was completely enveloped in a radiant,
sparkling glow.

While Justin stood agape, their eyes locked again, their right
hands met in mid-air, and they began to dance slowly, round and
round in a circle. From out of nowhere, the most beautiful music
burst forth and filled the air. Captivated, Justin watched as this
golden couple danced round and round in a trance-like state.
Round and round, round and round. The beat of the music
increased faster and faster and they kept time with it, spinning
faster and faster, round and round, faster and faster. Justin
couldn't believe how fast they were spinning. Round and round,
faster and faster, faster and faster. He was getting dizzy watching
them. They were spinning so fast now that he could no longer tell
where one began and the other left off. All you could see was a
whirling spiral of intense golden light. Then there was a huge
bright flash, like lightening. It knocked Justin down and he hit his
head on the willow tree.

When he came to, he felt groggy and there was a painful knot
on his head. He heard giggling and looked down to see Pitter and
Alaina standing there. The wedding clothes were gone. The music
had stopped. There was no sign of anything he had just seen. Had
he imagined it?

"What happened?" he asked, rubbing the sore spot on his
head.

"We're married!" they cried gleefully in unison.

"Married? Just like that?"

"Just like that!" Pitter said. "Fairies don't play the games
humans do. We know when our hearts are true. When it is time, it

is time!"

"So, what now?" Justin asked.

"Now we must go and build our summer house." Alaina answered.

"You may come if you'd like." Pitter said.

"Yes! Yes! I'd like that."

Off they went searching for the perfect spot. Justin trailed a bit behind. After all, he was a human, he thought. How was he to know exactly what kind of spot they were looking for. Without warning, Pitter wheeled around and fixed Justin with penetrating eyes while Alaina tripped on ahead. "What's the matter with you?" Justin demanded.

"What were you thinking just now? Tell me quick."

Hesitantly, Justin replied, "That I'm human, so I have no idea what kind of place you're looking for."

Pitter clapped his hands together and spun around twice, then leaped in the air and tapped his heels.

"Oh joy, oh joy!" he cried. "I did it. I read your mind. I actually *heard* your thoughts. That's *never* happened before. I'm growing up. I'm moving on. I'm getting more of my powers!"

"Over here." Alaina called. "Pitter! Justin! Come look. I've found the perfect spot."

"Not a word to Alaina." Pitter cautioned. "She believes I already have all the powers I need." Then he winked.

Justin shook his head and said, "You're impossible, Pitter. And you should know by now, I never tell your secrets."

"I know!" Pitter laughed. "You're an exemplary friend. Now, let's go build Alaina a house."

Alaina had indeed, found the perfect spot. In a very remote area in the Deep Woods, she had discovered mound after mound of soft, velvety emerald green moss sheltered by several venerable old trees. She had selected a particularly brilliant green patch and there they found her sitting contentedly in the center of it beaming from ear to ear.

"Here," she trilled, "is where we shall live our first summer together, Pitter. Isn't it marvelous!"

Pitter agreed wholeheartedly and set to work gathering small fallen branches covered in gray green fungi. With these they made a framework on top of the patch Alaina had chosen. Next they scouted the forest floor for pieces of bark for the walls and the roof. Before attaching the walls to the framework, they cut out window openings on two sides and an opening for a door in front. They chose a piece of bark for the roof that curved up along the sides. The idea was to provide shelter from the rain and insects and still allow cool breezes to flow through.

With a deft hand, Pitter wove a door of willow branches and set it in place, adding a little latch. Alaina surveyed the progress and declared something was missing. Then inspired she said, "Beetle curtains! We need beetle curtains!" And she scurried off.

Justin looked at Pitter. "Beetle curtains?" he asked.

"Yes, they're all the rage with the fairy ladies. My mother has them."

"What are they?"

"You'll see!"

Soon Alaina was back with a clutch of skeletonized leaves in her hands. "Humans think Japanese Beetles are horrid," she said. "But I think they're beautiful creatures and they make the loveliest curtains!" With that she hurried inside with her prize and immediately hung one at each window. Then looking up, she added one to each opening where the roof bowed up away from the walls. Excitedly, she rushed back outside. With hands behind her back, she tiptoed all around the little house inspecting it. Pitter stood back and watched, arms folded over his chest which was swelling ever larger with pride. At last Alaina pronounced herself satisfied and Pitter let out a jubilant shout.

It's a fine house." Justin said. "But I don't think I'll come in for tea!" With that they all laughed uproariously.

Then Pitter scooped Alaina up in his arms and whisked her across the threshold of their new home. Turning, he winked at Justin. "See you tomorrow." he said. With that he wheeled around and kicked the door shut. Completely flabbergasted at how their afternoon had turned out, Justin walked back through the woods and headed home, the tinkling sound of their laughter ringing in his ears.

Chapter Eleven

Justin didn't see Pitter and Alaina the next day after all - or the next. A weather disturbance had moved in during the night. It poured and poured. Justin and Faye were relieved to know that Pitter wasn't out in the woods alone. They knew the rain often made him melancholy.

But not this time! Pitter was having the time of his life. He and Alaina had quickly settled into a state of domestic bliss. The time slipped away like vapor in a breeze. They took great delight in their quaint little house with its fashionable beetle curtains and its plush carpet of velvety green moss. The old trees surrounding their home provided a canopy of protection from the worst of the rain and wind. Inside, they were warm and snug and deliriously happy. From time to time, they would venture out. (Fairies never like to be indoors for long, no matter how comfortable the surroundings are). On these occasions they would race pieces of bark down little rivulets of water or play tag with the chipmunks and toads taking shelter under the skunk cabbage umbrellas. And all the while they talked and talked - sharing their lives, learning all they could about each other. It was as if Mother Nature had intervened with the rain to create a circle of privacy around them. It was a moment out of time, when two hearts learned to sing love's song in one voice, and two minds set a single course for the same objectives. It was in essence, a perfect fairy honeymoon.

The sun had just broken through the clouds on the afternoon of the third day when Justin heard tapping at the kitchen window. There was Pitter and Alaina, hovering in mid air while holding hands. They looked ecstatic. Justin and Faye hurried outside to greet them. The pride in Pitter's voice as he introduced Alaina to Faye was unmistakable.

"Look!" Alaina said, holding Pitter's hand up for them to see. "There's only one left. Just the little blue one in the center." Justin and Faye marveled at the disappearance of all but one of the Circles of Attunement.

"I've been *very* good for him, haven't I?" Alaina glowed as she said this. It was more a statement than a question.

"Yes, you have." Justin and Faye said enthusiastically.

Pitter only gazed at her with adoring eyes and squeezed her hand. He needed no words to say what was in his heart. But he needed to make one thing perfectly clear about the circles.

"It's that last little blue one that will be the most difficult to erase. It requires sacrificing your own safety and well-being without a moment's hesitation to save another. Such circumstances are not likely to come along any time soon, nor would I want them too. Then remembering one of the main purposes for their visit, Pitter changed the subject by saying, "Incidentally, we came to tell you that we are leaving tomorrow."

Faye's face withered with bewilderment. Justin cried out in protest, "No! No! You can't go!"

"Don't worry," Pitter answered, hastening to set their minds at ease. "We'll be back in a week or two. And we won't be alone! We'll have a whole family of fairies with us. Alaina's family.

Faye burst into tears of joy. Justin danced a jig. At last the woods and gardens would be filled with fairies - after all these years. When they finally collected themselves, Pitter continued.

"Alaina's family is in desperate need of a new home.   The

humans are bulldozing down their woods and fairy mounds for a new development. Soon all the land they inhabited will be covered in asphalt parking lots and concrete buildings. They have moved to a tiny little park in a city nearby while scouts search for a new place. Alaina is one of those scouts. She found The Land of Faye only by chance. Like others before her, she was very distrustful of it because it seemed *too* perfect. The absence of fairies alarmed her. She was preparing to move on and look for another spot when we found her. Lucky for all of us, we were not too late. We have Grand Oak to thank for that. In the meantime," Pitter said, changing the subject, "Alaina and I would like you to join us later in the Deep Woods for a little festivity in the moonlight. The Fairy Candles are blooming gloriously. You must see how wonderfully they illuminate a fairy ring. It will be a perfect night for dancing and we all have much to celebrate."

"We certainly do!" Faye agreed, thrilled at the news that more fairies would be coming soon. "Justin and I will be delighted to attend. I'll bring some sweets and we'll have a grand party."

Pitter and Alaina took their leave and Faye busied herself in the kitchen. She made an aromatic rose geranium cake and some honey lavender cookies. Then, remembering Pitter's love of rosemary, she quickly stirred up a batch of rosemary shortbread. She cut each confection in diminutive pieces and placed them on a small plate of her best crystal. She had always heard that fairies loved crystal. Then she took the tiny antique tea service from its place in the cupboard and wrapped it ever so carefully in tissue paper. When everything was ready, she and Justin set out for the Deep Woods.

They had no trouble finding their way under the glowing light of a full moon. The air was calm and pleasantly warm and the woodlands exuded a delicious fragrance. Along the way, they met a raccoon who bowed decorously as they passed. A doe and her fawn stopped to gaze at them and nod a greeting. A group of hawk moths, busy sipping nectar from evening primroses, entertained them briefly with an aerial acrobatic performance, then zipped back to their dinners. It was all quite breathtaking.

Justin, afraid that he might not remember the exact location of Pitter and Alaina's home, had no trouble finding it after all. Pitter was busy sweeping the moss outside the door with a mop of wild bergamot when they arrived. Relishing his new role as host, he called Alaina, who burst through the door before he could even finish her name. Faye complimented them on their lovely home and praised Alaina for her unique choice of curtains. Then she presented them with the gifts in her basket. They were touched and delighted with the tea service. Pitter quickly produced a little gourd jug that held a delicate flavored rosewater. He filled the four tiny cups and made a toast. The crystal plate was passed and they all sampled the tasty little sweets.

On cue from Alaina, four fat toads came hopping out from under a wild rose bush. Each was carrying a small musical instrument. One had a flute made from a woody stalk of lovage. Another had a small gourd fiddle with spider web strings. The third carried a clutch of striped love-in-a-mist pods. As he walked by, he shook the pods in Justin's direction. The dried seeds inside created a rhythmic, swishing sound like a maraca. This was really a first. Love-in-a-mist pods in the percussion section! Bringing up the rear, was a dapper fellow sporting a polka dot tie and an acorn drum. Considering the size of the acorn, Justin was sure it must be one of Grand Oak's offspring.

The toads took their places at the edge of a large expanse of moss surrounded by stands of black cohosh in full bloom. The tall plants with their plump, furry white spikes reaching heavenward, captured the muted glow of the moonbeams filtering through the towering treetops. Anyone coming up on this bewitching scene, would quickly understand why these stately, luminous plants have long been called fairy candles.

Raising up on their hind legs, the toads tuned their instruments and began to play. Faye and Justin could not believe their eyes - or their ears. It was a most incredible sight. The toad trio belted out one lively tune after another as Pitter and Alaina danced round and round. Faye and Justin did their best to keep up with them, being ever so careful not to accidentally step on their tiny host and hostess.

Before long, they all became aware that they were surrounded by glowing eyes and thumping feet, as forest creatures came out of the deep shadows and joined the party. They kept perfect time, clapping and tapping their paws. And just as the celebration was beginning to break up, Owl flew in to offer his congratulations to the newlyweds. It was a grand evening, filled with a fairy enchantment unlike anything The Land of Faye had experienced in a very long time.

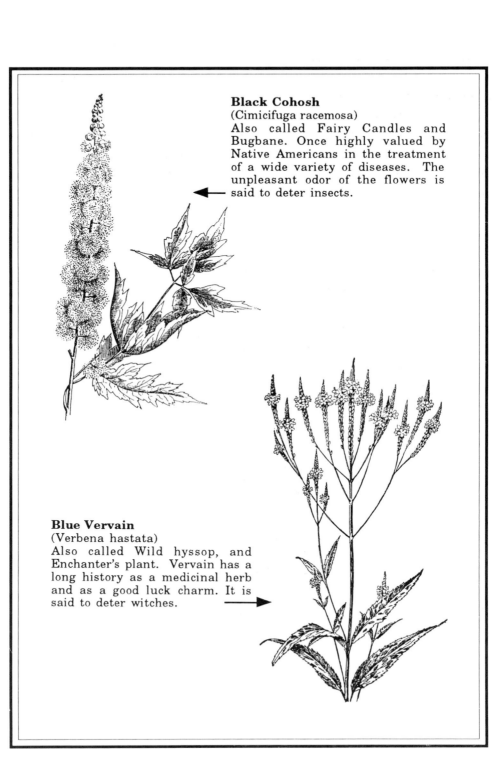

Black Cohosh
(Cimicifuga racemosa)
Also called Fairy Candles and Bugbane. Once highly valued by Native Americans in the treatment of a wide variety of diseases. The unpleasant odor of the flowers is said to deter insects.

Blue Vervain
(Verbena hastata)
Also called Wild hyssop, and Enchanter's plant. Vervain has a long history as a medicinal herb and as a good luck charm. It is said to deter witches.

Chapter Twelve

When morning came, Pitter and Alaina were well on their way to find her family. Faye scanned the calendar and realized there were things she and Justin needed to take care of in the city. Time had certainly slipped away without her realizing it. They packed the car, closed up the house and headed for Justin's home. His parents would be returning in a couple of weeks and school would be starting shortly after that. There were clothes and supplies to buy, and the house needed a good airing out and cleaning.

It all took more time than they had bargained for and a whole week passed before they were able to head back to The Land of Faye. Both were filled with anxious wonder about what they would find when they got there. It was all they could talk about. The trip seemed to take longer than it had ever taken before. They were ecstatic when they finally turned into the long lane. On both sides, blooming wildflowers greeted them. Orange black-eyed Susans and blue chicory, white Queen Anne's lace and red cardinal flowers, purple coneflowers and yellow goldenrods, all combined to create a brilliant tapestry of color. And here and there, peeking out from leaves and blossoms, were fairies waving to them. They were flabbergasted and so distracted that Faye almost drove the car into a tree. When they got to the house, Pitter and Alaina were waiting for them on the steps of the front porch.

"So what do you think?" Pitter asked gleefully. "Are there enough fairies for you now?"

"Oh my, yes!" Faye exclaimed. "This is just the most wondrous thing! How can I ever repay you?"

Alaina and Pitter exchanged a strange glance, then burst into embarrassed snickering.

"Well, since you asked," Alaina began. "We were wondering if you would be my midwife."

"Midwife?" Faye couldn't believe her ears. "You're expecting a baby? When?"

"Any day really!" Pitter said. "And I remembered you told me once that you had trained as a midwife years ago and have delivered human babies. It would be a comfort to know we can call on you."

"Oh my! Well, of course!" Faye replied, flustered by this unexpected turn of events.

"Wait a minute!" Justin interrupted. "What do you mean, any day? Even I know it takes nine months to have a baby. It's only been . . ."

"You must remember, Justin," Pitter reminded him. "Fairy time is different from human time in most things. Nothing takes as long for us as it does for you."

"Wow!" Justin said. "If I were a fairy, I'll bet I could finish school in a month instead of having to spend years and years!"

They all laughed and Faye rumpled his hair. "You are such a darling dear," she said tenderly.

"It's interesting that you call him that." Pitter said with a hint of sadness in his voice. "My mother and grandmother used to always call me their darling dear. I miss that."

Justin quickly brought his friend's attention back to the baby. "I can't imagine what a fairy baby will look like. I hope it's a girl. I've always, *always* wanted a little sister. That would just be the most awesome thing!"

"And what would you name this little sister?" Alaina asked.

Without a moment's hesitation, Justin said, "Andraleena!"

"That's a lovely name." Alaina said, repeating it softly several times. "Whatever made you choose it?"

"I don't really know. I've never heard anyone called Andraleena. I just thought of it one night and liked the way it sounded. It reminds me of something you might hear in one of those pretty love songs - though I'm not real crazy about *love* songs." They all laughed again. Then Pitter and Alaina said their goodbyes and went off to join the other fairies for a day of work and frolic.

The next morning, Pitter arrived early and invited Justin to go for a walk in the Old Forest. "So much has happened in the last few weeks," he said. "I miss the time we used to spend together."

"It's not the same anymore," Justin said. "You seem so grown up now. Let's face it. You *are* grown up. You have a wife, a baby on the way, and now a whole family of other fairies to look after. Soon, I'll have to go back to school in the city. Everything's changed."

"Yes! And soon Alaina and I and the other fairies will have to go underground for the winter."

"At least you won't be spending the winter alone like you feared. That would have been the worst thing."

"Well, not the worst thing? There are other things that can happen to fairies that are worse than spending the winter alone."

"Like what? What's the worst thing?"

Pitter's face grew somber. When he answered, it was in a hushed, solemn voice that aroused Justin's curiosity even more.

"Being Betwixt Between." Pitter said quietly.

"Betwixt Between? What does that mean? Hey, Pitter, I made a rhyme!"

Pitter shot an angry look at Justin that startled him.

"Never, *never*," he said emphatically, "Make a joke of those two words. Don't *ever* say them lightly!"

"**I'm sorry.**" Justin apologized. He was shaken at his friend's outburst.

"**You had no way of knowing.** Betwixt Between signifies a sad, sad time for fairies. It is a time when, because of circumstances they cannot control, they must leave their home and find another. To put it another way, it means 'we can no longer stay here, but we have no place to go.' We are lost in between two places with no idea how it will end. Like Alaina's family. Nothing strikes fear in a fairy's heart like those two words."

"Have *you* ever been 'Betwixt Between'?"

"Not me. But my family has - many, many years ago." Pitter hesitated briefly and then told Justin the story of the fairy stones and the place they had once lived. When he finished, Justin was speechless.

"I might as well tell you the rest." Pitter continued. "Remember when I told you and your grandmother about the night my grandfather gave me the Circles of Attunement?"

"Yes."

"Well, I never really explained why. Justin's eyes grew larger and larger as Pitter told the story of goading Gil into telling why he was so unkempt and mocking him when he said it was because they were 'Betwixt Between'.

"I reacted like you just did." Pitter said, his voice filled with shame. "I made a silly rhyme out of it. 'Betwixt Between'. What does it mean.' I started to chant it over and over. Then I added a jig to the chant and danced and danced around Gil. Like this." All the while Pitter was telling the story, he was demonstrating the jig to Justin.

Justin found it hard to believe his friend could ever have been so thoughtless. He could see now why his grandfather had become so angry with him and had punished him so severely. It was a terrible thing he had done.

Pitter stopped. He could see the look of disillusionment on his friend's face. He should never have told him. They sat in silence for a while, each mulling over what had been said. At last, Pitter rose to leave. "Now you know! I don't *ever* want to speak of this again!"

Then remembering something, he stopped. "Did I tell you, when the humans from across the wide sea came to that valley years later, they found the land of the tear stones. The First People told them our story and how we had to flee to find a new home free of the memories. The tear stones became lucky charms to the new ones. To this day, they still collect them and call them fairy stones." With that, he turned and disappeared toward his home in the Deep Woods.

Cardinal Flower
(Lobelia cardinalis)
Also called Red Lobelia. It's
striking red blossoms are a favorite
of hummingbirds. It was once used
medicinally by Native Americans.

Purple Coneflower
(Echinacea purpurea)
Widely used as a medicinal herb by
Native Americans. Modern research
has validated some of its health
benefits. Long valued as a garden
flower that attracts butterflies.

Chapter Thirteen

In The Golden Valley, things had gone from bad to worse. Rumors had been flying about some sort of massive structure the humans had built at the end of the valley. Patter, still overwhelmed with his duties as King, continued to dismiss the concerns being raised. The outer guards grumbled among themselves, questioning his competence. The Prime Minister and the courtiers shook their heads in dismay at his ineptness. Even those who had believed Pitter irresponsible and unfit to be king were having second thoughts. And if these weren't problems enough, heavy rains in the last week had flooded streams in the valley and caused walls of mud and rock to come crashing down from the hillsides. Nerves were frayed to the breaking point.

But at last, things seemed to be taking a turn for the better. The weather had cleared sometime before sunset and Patter had decreed that the night be spent in dancing and revelry. Such declarations seemed to be the only times the fairies liked him. It was obvious now that no one respected him. The confidence he had felt earlier in the summer had given way to self doubt. He longed for Pitter's return and to have this heavy mantle of leadership taken from him. He was weary of trying to be what he wasn't.

The music and dancing were like a tonic to the little fairy kingdom. Laughter filled the air and tensions flitted off into the moonlight. Everyone seemed to forget their cares. All except Lyla. As she had done night after night since Pitter's disappearance, she watched and waited for her errant boy to return. While the other fairies played their melodious flutes and danced with gleeful abandon, she stood in the shadows looking heavenward, hoping for a small purple glimmer to appear. Over and over she had to press her magic wand tight against her chest to keep her heart from falling to pieces. Where was her charmer - her mischievous boy? She worried, as all mothers do and have ever done, that he had fallen to harm.

"Do you see anything, Dear? Pitter's grandmother asked, coming up to stand by Lyla.

"No - not a glimmer. Not a sign." she sighed. "Where is our darling boy, Momma? I miss his jokes, his laughter, his naughty, almost-human ways."

"I know, Dear." Grandmother replied wistfully. "So do I. So do I." And they both clasped their wands to their chests to keep their hearts from breaking in two.

"It will soon be daylight, Lyla," Grandmother said, collecting herself. "No use to stand watch anymore tonight. You need your rest. Patter is here to take you home." Then with a sweeping motion, Grandmother tapped Lyla's head lightly with her wand and a cloud of shimmering, silver dust enveloped her.

"Rest well my child," Grandmother said. And Lyla knew she would. The sleeping dust never failed to bring about a deep, deep slumber. Only two things could wake her - the lullaby of a setting sun and the thunder from the Gong of Great Calamity. And *it* had not been heard since long before Pitter and Patter were born. Drowsy from the sleep dust, Lyla took Patter's hand and allowed him to lead her home and tuck her in. Before she drifted into a sound sleep, she thought she saw Pitter dancing a jig and chanting a disturbing rhyme. Then sleep engulfed her and closed the door on her tormented thoughts.

Throughout the valley, fairies broke their dancing, packed

their flutes away, replaced the fairy candles on their stems, gathered the wee ones from their nurses and headed off to bed. A faint sliver of light was hovering on the horizon. Welcoming birds songs could be heard in the distance heralding the approaching dawn. Soon the valley would belong to the dayworld. One by one, they all fell blissfully off to sleep - oblivious to the looming crisis that was only hours away.

Shortly after daybreak, a major storm system moved in over The Golden Valley -- and stalled.   Torrents of rain poured down. Unbeknownst to the slumbering fairy clan, the flood gates had been closed on a massive manmade structure that would transform their surroundings forever. The Golden Valley, the place they had called home for hundreds of years, was destined to become the Leisure Time Lake - and much sooner than anyone had predicted.

Faye and Justin took their lunch into the living room so they could watch the latest news reports on television.   It had been storming now for over six hours and while rain amounts over The Land of Faye had been light, other areas of the state were experiencing torrential downpours. Up to six inches had already fallen in some places, swelling rivers and streams and causing extensive flooding. They watched with interest as another special weather update came on. News crews had been dispatched to the hardest hit regions. A reporter was now telling the anchor desk of current conditions in one of the areas most effected.

"Jeb, we're here live at the Leisure Time Dam. Rain has been coming down at a rate of one inch per hour. With the ground already saturated from storms earlier in the week, there's no place for the water to go. But the news isn't all bad. Only yesterday, the engineers closed the flood gates on this multimillion dollar project at the mouth of Leisure Valley.   The resulting back up of water from rivers, streams and hillside run-off will create the new Leisure Time Lake and spare residents downstream from what would otherwise have been a major flood."

The camera panned the gigantic structure as the reporter continued. "While it had been expected to take days for the lake to reach optimum level, the storm has accelerated the process. The water is rising at record rates. Here's an interesting little side note for you, Jeb. Old timers in the area tell me there's a legend that fairies used to live in the remote areas of this valley. In the local folklore this is called 'The Golden Valley' - (chuckle, chuckle!). If there are any fairies *still* around, they had better have some sturdy boats and life vests today. Back to you, Jeb."

Justin was out of his chair and racing for the door. "I've got to tell Pitter," he cried.

"Wait, get your raincoat. I'll go with you." Faye shouted.

"I don't have time." he yelled back as he rushed headlong out into the rain.

Faye grabbed her raincoat and a small bag she had waiting on the table and hurried after him. He was already out of sight. The rain was heavier now and it was hard to see where she was going but she pushed on. Brambles snagged her clothes and mud soon caked her shoes. She slogged on, tripping over limbs and twigs that littered the way.

At the same time in the Deep Woods, another crisis was unfolding. Alaina was about to give birth and she was afraid that things were not as they should be. Her apprehension sent Pitter into a state of panic. After making her as comfortable as possible and showering her with reassurances that he would be back quickly with Faye, he hurried out.

He realized immediately that his fragile wings would be of little use in the pouring rain and he began to run.   Not far from his little home, he encountered a large object blocking his way. Swiftly, he started to climb over it. It felt soft and had a distinctly human smell. Brushing the water from his eyes, he looked around at the mound he was standing on and was shocked to realize it was Justin laying flat on the ground.

Just then, Pitter heard someone running toward him shouting Justin's name. He watched as Faye came charging through the underbrush at breakneck speed. She stopped abruptly when she saw Justin, then fell to her knees by his side, calling his name over and over trying to rouse him.

"I think he tripped and hit his head on this tree trunk. We must get him out of the rain and check his injuries." Pitter's voice was filled with concern as he sized up the situation.

"But how?" Faye asked.

At the same moment, Pitter remembered why he was out in the rain in the first place and interrupted.

"I was on my way to get you, Faye. Alaina is about to have the baby and we're afraid there might be a problem."

This news only added to Faye's anxiety. "But we can't deliver a baby outside in the rain! What are we to do?"

Pitter thought a second, then squeezed his eyes shut, hoping against hope that he could summon the powers that had alluded him before. A streak of lightening split the air and a crashing cacophony of thunder reverberated through the woods. At that same instant, Pitter's wand appeared in his hand. Gleaming with a newfound confidence, he tapped Justin, then Faye. In a flash, they were both fairy-size. Pitter could hardly contain his excitement. "I did it, Faye! I actually *did* it! I've never been able to shape-shift anyone before, but look at this!" Then remembering his friend's dilemma, Pitter scooped Justin's now tiny limp form into his arms and they scurried off to the shelter of the fairy house.

Once inside, Pitter gently laid Justin on the mossy carpet

and scanned him with his wand. "He will be fine in a few minutes." Pitter reported. "There is a bump on his head, but nothing serious. The fall only stunned him."

Relieved, Faye immediately turned her attention to Alaina. Here too, there was good news. The birth was progressing normally and there was no cause for worry. Quickly, Faye extracted sprigs of blue vervain from the small bag she had with her and began hanging it over each window and the door. "We're not taking any chances with your precious wee one." she said. "If there are any Evil Ones in these woods, which I seriously doubt, they won't come near your home. They have an immense aversion to blue vervain." Alaina relaxed and began to hum a fairy lullaby. It was obvious she was in good hands and had nothing to fear after all.

A soft moaning brought their focus back to Justin. He was starting to sit up, his hand rubbing his head. Still dazed, he looked around in disbelief. "What's going on? Where am I?"

"You're in my home." Pitter answered. "You had a fall. And I *did* it, Justin! I made you my size! I have my shape-shifting powers!" He danced around joyfully a moment, then froze, a puzzled look furrowing his forehead. Looking at first Faye and then Justin, he asked, "Come to think of it, what in the world were the two of you doing out in the rain, anyway?"

"Oh, goodness! In all the upset over Justin and Alaina, I completely forgot." Faye stammered. "Pitter, we have *awful* news. The Golden Valley is about to be completely flooded. They've built a dam at the end of the valley. And now all of this rain is causing the water to rise at record rates. We saw it on television."

Pitter's face was ashen as he took this all in. "It's day time. The fairies are all asleep. They won't even know. I must warn them! I must try to save them! But that's impossible? I don't even know how to find The Golden Valley from here!"

Justin was on his feet now. "We must find a way. You can't fly in this, that's for sure. And Owl won't fly in daylight." He scratched his head as options raced through his mind. "I know! Mother Duck and her husband. They would take us. They said they would do *anything* for you."

"Yes, yes, that might work. But what do you mean - *us?*"

"I'm going with you, Pitter." Justin said emphatically. "I know where The Golden Valley is now. I always knew but never realized it until I saw the newscast today. We call it by another name - Leisure Valley. I can lead you there."

Pitter hesitated a second, looking anxiously at Faye and Alaina. How could he leave his Alaina at a time like this?

Alaina sensed his concern and rushed to reassure him. "I'll be in very capable hands with Faye. You *must* do everything you can to save your family. We'll be here waiting for you when you return. I wouldn't have it any other way."

The rain had tapered off to a light sprinkle by the time Pitter and Justin arrived at the edge of the lake where Mother Duck and the Drake lived with their children. As soon as the ducks heard about the frightening situation in The Golden Valley, they were eager to help. Pitter and Justin climbed on board the ducks' backs, locking their arms tightly around their necks. A few final instructions to their children, and the ducks lifted off. They knew about flooding and how quickly water can rise. There was not a second to lose.

Once airborne, Justin gave directions based on the map and landmarks he had seen on the news report. They had no idea what they would find once they got there. Mother Duck suggested that they would surely need extra help if they were forced to rescue the entire band of fairies. Pitter and Justin readily agreed. As they raced on, the two ducks began squawking out a plea for assistance.

From lake and stream and garden pond they came, answering the distress call. First three ducks, then five, then eight - the numbers swelled as the ragged V-shaped rescue squad sped northward into an increasing barrage of pouring rain. By the time they reached The Golden Valley, their ranks had grown to seventy-two ducks.

Meanwhile, in The Golden Valley, the outer guards had sounded the Gong of Great Calamity. Groggy from being awakened from a deep sleep the fairies rushed through pouring rain and puddles of water to their appointed places on the old oak log at the Meeting Ring. Intense fear gripped them. Only impending disaster would justify the use of the gong.

Patter paced nervously on the squishy moss, scanning the group to make sure everyone was accounted for. Then, his voice shaking with fear and helplessness, he told them what the outer guards had seen.

It was the sound that had alerted them first. A soft, swishing, sloshing noise that grew louder and louder. Then brilliant flashes of lightening had illuminated the valley floor just below the large woods. What they saw in that brief glimpse struck fear in their hearts. The entire valley was a dark, menacing, swirling mass of water. Terror-stricken, they watched as the water level spread up and up, wider and wider. Only a few more inches and the water would breach the small slope dividing the fairy woodlands from the lower portion of the valley. Knowing the sleeping fairies were only minutes away from being drowned, they dashed to sound the Gong of Great Calamity.

Patter had no sooner finished telling them this, than a loud roaring sound threw everyone into a frenzy. Ominous fingers of water could be seen rushing their way into the Meeting Ring. They

112

collected, pooled, and eddied, lapping up everything in their path. Not a moment too soon, Patter ran for the log and quickly scampered up. Those seated in the lower tiers, climbed higher. The water streamed around, then under the log. The old log shuttered as it was wrenched lose from its mooring of moss and fungi. Fairies clutched each other tightly trying to maintain their balance as the log lifted, then rolled slightly. They screamed as they floated precariously, tipping back and forth. There was no escape. Their wings were useless in the pelting rain and fairy powers were no match for such devastating circumstances. The log swayed and bobbed, occasionally bumping into trees gasping their last breaths. It was only a matter of time, before the log rolled over completely, or filled with water and sank. They were doomed. In a blinding, universal realization, they knew there was something even worse than being Betwixt Between. Loud squawks pierced their consciousness and in unison, they looked up. A large flock of ducks circled overhead.

With the help of Mother Duck and the Drake, Pitter and Justin had instantly assessed the situation below and formulated a valiant plan. One by one, the ducks swooped down to the teetering log where they hovered momentarily stretching a wing out for the fairies to grasp. Hand over hand, the terrified fairies scaled this feathered lifeline until they reached the safety of the duck's neck. Once securely on board, the duck then glided gracefully over the rising water, lifted back up into the sky and headed south. Anxiously, Pitter and Justin watched as the harrowing rescue proceeded. It was a slow, nerve-racking process. Only when the last fairy was safely in the air and Pitter had confirmed that his mother, brother and grandmother were accounted for, did he heave a sigh of relief. Solemnly, he saluted the now inundated Golden Valley, then signaled Mother Duck to follow Justin and the others - *home*.

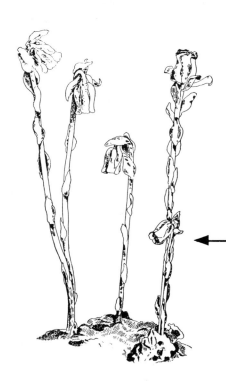

Indian Pipe
(Monotropa uniflora)
Also called Fairy Smoke and
American Iceplant. It was once
used medicinally particularly to
treat inflamation of the eyes. A
saprophyte, it relies on decaying
matter for survival.

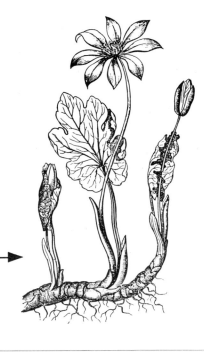

Bloodroot
(Sanguinaria canadensis)
Once a favorite dye plant and
medicinal herb. Native Americans
used it to decorate their bodies and
belongings. The root is rich in a
blood red juice, hence the name.

Chapter Fourteen

As Pitter and Justin had agreed, Justin led the rescue party back to The Land of Faye. Once there, he took the bedraggled, exhausted fairies to the house and guided them indoors. They were too stunned by all that had happened to question or resist. Promising to return soon, he left them to tidy up and rest, and headed off to the Deep Woods. He was anxious to learn how Alaina was doing.

The tiny house was bursting with jubilation when he arrived. Pitter and Alaina were dancing round and round. Their faces radiated happiness. In the center of the room sat Faye rocking a milkweed pod cradle. She beamed at Justin with pride as he tiptoed closer to take a peek. Inside, was the most beautiful baby he had ever seen. So very, very tiny, and yet the epitome of total perfection. He smiled. The lovely little face looked back at him with arresting violet eyes and smiled too. He was overwhelmed with a kind of love he had never felt before. This must be what it feels like to have a little sister, he thought.

"So, what do you think of our beautiful daughter?" Pitter asked, although he already knew the answer.

"She is the prettiest thing I ever saw in my life!" Justin exclaimed. "Have you named her yet?"

"Yes!" Alaina said softly. "Pitter and I have decided to call her Andraleena - just for you."

Justin blinked, then blinked again, as tears welled up in his eyes. "Andraleena!" he repeated tenderly.

Touched, Alaina and Pitter put their arms around him. "It's the least we can do after all you and your grandmother have done for us and for our families. You said you always longed for a baby sister named Andraleena. We want you to think of our dear little wee one as the sister you never had. She could not have a better big brother, unless of course, he was a fairy."

Justin was speechless, awed by the implications of this sacred moment. He reached out his hand to Andraleena. She grasped his finger and held on to it tightly. He felt an odd tingling pass from her tiny fingertips into his, and a profound awareness slip into his consciousness. They were now linked by a bond that could never be broken. A sense of enormous responsibility and devotion filled him and he welcomed it. What a magical summer this had turned out to be.

Later, after Alaina and Andraleena had drifted off into a blissful nap, Pitter returned Justin and Faye to their proper sizes. The rain had stopped and the clouds were beginning to break up.

"I would like to see my mother and Patter." Pitter said. "I want them to know I am safe and to meet Alaina and Andraleena. But after all that has happened, I'm sure the others won't care to see me. I let them all down."

"But you saved them!" Justin objected.

"So did you! Besides, they never would have been in that predicament if I had been responsible in the first place - if I had been King. I can take little credit for rescuing them, when my own actions put them in jeopardy in the first place."

"You're being far too hard on yourself." Faye interjected. "But we respect your wishes. What would you like us to do?"

"I'd like you to bring Patter and my mother here right away, but please don't tell them or the others anything about me. I want to tell them about everything that has happened myself."

Faye and Justin could not believe their eyes when they arrived back home and walked inside. Two makeshift clothes lines had been strung from one side of the kitchen to the other. A rainbow of colorful tunics and frocks filled each sagging strand. Faye smiled to herself as she realized they had found the ball of string she used for tying up bunches of herbs. But where were the fairies? They must be close by. After all, they don't have any clothes on! Faye and Justin looked at each other sheepishly as awareness sunk in. *No clothes on!*

No wonder! They must be mortified at having two humans intrude on them when they're all in the buff. The only polite and sensible thing to do was to give them their privacy. Faye reached her hand up to feel the tiny clothes dangling from the lines. They felt dry and soft, with just a slight trace of crispness - something freshly starched and ironed. No wonder they always looked so neat and well-groomed.

"Please excuse our intrusion, dears," Faye called out to them. "We're very sorry we startled you. There is nothing to fear. We'll just step outside until you're dressed. Your clothes are dry now." With that, Justin and Faye went back out and waited on the porch. Instantly, there was a flurry of chattering and bustling activity indoors - then silence. The door opened and a small fairy child beckoned them to come in. Fairies were everywhere. Some perched on top of cabinets and picture frames, while others sat primly on the couch and chairs, on the floor and on the kitchen table. And all their shiny little faces looked expectantly at Faye. She was totally overwhelmed.

She quickly introduced herself and Justin and welcomed them all to The Land of Faye. She showed them the map on the wall and they all took turns squeezing in close together to look at it as she told them about the woods, the Old Forest, the herb garden and all the other wonderful places there were for fairies to reside.

"You see," Justin pointed out. "There is no reason for you to worry about being Betwixt Between." The fairies all exchanged furtive glances and shocked gasps wondering how this human boy could know about Betwixt Between. Regretting his choice of words and wanting to dispel their worries, he forged on. "This place is a perfect haven for fairies. There is an abundance of plants and trees and shrubs here that should make you very happy. This is your home for as long as you want it to be."

A relieved, delighted murmuring swept through the throng of fairies. Then Patter stepped forward. Justin and Faye knew it was him instantly. He was the exact image of Pitter. "We thank you for your hospitality." he said. "We have many questions, as you can imagine, but I'm sure they will all be answered in good time. For now, we are extremely weary of being cooped up indoors and wish to be outside to explore this place you call The Land of Faye."

Faye opened the door and held it wide. "You are free to leave anytime. Please make yourself at home. You can't imagine how happy I am to have you here."

The fairies poured out into the fresh air and sunshine, twirling and spinning, running hither and yon, investigating everything and marveling at it all. Patter hesitated and was joined by a slender fairy with earnest eyes that reminded Justin of Pitter.

"Are you Pitter's mother?" Justin asked.

"Yes!" Lyla said breathlessly. "You know Pitter? You know my darling dear? Is he here? Where is he?"

"Yes." Faye assured her quickly. "We know Pitter and he is here. He wants to see you. Would you like to see him?"

"Of course!" Lyla answered incredulously. "I have longed for nothing else since he disappeared. Why is he here? Why did he never come home?"

"It is for Pitter to tell you the answers to your questions." Justin said. "We will take you to him."

Pitter was pacing back and forth in front of his little home, when Faye and Justin arrived with Patter and his mother. Not wanting to interfere, Justin and Faye left the three alone. Lyla and Patter were so thrilled to see Pitter that they almost knocked him down as they rushed at him with arms outstretched. There were hugs, and hugs, and more hugs. Revelation after revelation quickly followed. Pitter shared the events of his summer and they shared their's. He was shocked to learn that his grandfather's passing was not his fault, that Patter hated being King, and that all the other fairies wanted him to return and lead them. It was an astounding turn of events.

He was trying very hard to absorb it all when Lyla cried out in surprise. "Pitter, the circles are gone. All the Circles of Attunement are gone!" She was looking intently at his hand which she was holding firmly in her own. Pitter had been so consumed by everything else, that he had not realized the last small blue circle had vanished. The twins stared at Pitter's hand, then at each other, and let out a loud whoop. Locking elbows, they danced a jig around their mother, shouting and laughing hysterically.

A faint cry from inside the house, caught Lyla's attention and she hushed the noisy pair. "Ah," Pitter said, grinning proudly. "It is time for you to meet two very special people in my new life. They are awake at last." They all tiptoed inside and Pitter quickly introduced Alaina to his mother and brother, and then presented Andraleena. It was an enormously joyous time. The happy reunion lasted well into the night.

Chapter Fifteen

The next morning found The Land of Faye in a whirlwind of activity. Word had been received that Justin's parents were arriving home ahead of schedule and wanted Justin and Faye to meet them at the airport the next day. Justin and Faye scurried around packing all of his belongings and getting everything ready. They would leave first thing in the morning.

The fairy clans were also hard at work. The first order of business was to install Pitter as the King of both families by unanimous agreement and with Patter's heartfelt blessing. Pitter accepted the crown with graciousness and humility, winning the hearts and allegiance of everyone. He immediately took charge, requesting the fairies to switch their sleeping patterns to nighttime temporarily. There was so much work to be done! There were seeds to look after, roots to tend, plants to tidy. They needed to make the most of what little time they had left in the outdoor world.

Some extensive investigation had turned up several more abandoned fairy mounds. Crews were dispatched to clean and sweep and refurbish the interiors, and make them ready for the long winter's rest. The summer was well on the wane and the air spirit spoke of a chill soon to come. Pitter had already decreed that when the preparations were complete, in a day or two, the fairies would retire to their underground homes.

Early that afternoon, Faye and Justin paid a farewell visit to Pitter and Alaina's little home. On greeting them, Pitter instantly shrank them to fairy-size and invited them in. It was a bittersweet gathering. They had all shared so much together and loved each other deeply. There were hugs and tears all around and fervent promises to reunite when spring came again. Pitter was already bursting with new ideas and plans for The Land of Faye.

Later, when Justin was loading some of his books into the car, Pitter appeared unexpectedly. "I know we already said our goodbyes but before you go, we have some unfinished business to take care of." he declared. Without another word, he headed off through the woods, signaling Justin to follow. Puzzled, Justin ran after him. When they arrived at the lake, they were greeted exuberantly by Mother Duck, the Drake, and their children.

"What brings you here today?" the Drake asked.

"Justin has longed all summer to ride the bullfrog," Pitter explained. "Today, he gets his wish."

Justin could barely contain his excitement. At Pitter's summoning, the hefty bullfrog swam amiably over to the edge of the lake where they were standing.

"So, you've finally got all your powers, eh?" the frog asked.

"Yes, I do." Pitter answered. And, as if to prove it, he tapped Justin. A bright flash of light, a waft of smoke, and Justin was standing eye-level with the frog.

"Yep, I'm impressed!" the old frog croaked approvingly. Then he hunkered down and allowed Justin to climb on his back. Pitter gave Justin the golden cord from around his waist and instructed him on how to hold it under the frog's neck. Then he slapped the frog lightly on the rump. The frog shot up into the air and then arced into the water. Breaking the surface with a deafening splash, he dove down, down, down into the cool, dark depths of the lake. Justin held on for dear life, his hair plastered like wet wings against the sides of his head. As Pitter had done all summer, he forced himself to keep his eyes open. Startled fish and tadpoles darted out of the way and bits of leaves and other debris whizzed past. The water stung his eyes and blurred his vision but it was still an unbelievable sight. The frog hit bottom, hesitated ever so briefly, then kicked off with his powerful legs, lunging upward through the murky depths. Up, up, up he zoomed. Kersplash! They broke through the rippling surface and sailed through the air in a long, perfect arc, coming to rest at Pitter's feet with a resounding *plunk*. Justin slid off, rolling on the ground in ecstasy. As soon as he caught his breath, he burst into uncontrollable laughter. At last, he exclaimed, "That was *absolutely awesome!* Thank you, Pitter."

"It's the least I could do!" Pitter said. Then with a tap on the shoulder, he changed Justin back to his original size.

Justin was dripping wet. In the fading sunlight, the air felt cooler and sent shivers running through him.

"You had better get home right away and out of those wet clothes." Pitter commanded. "We can't be sending you back to your parents sick." Then looking tenderly at Justin, he added, "I'm really going to miss you."

"I'll miss you too."

Silently, Pitter accompanied Justin to the edge of the woods.

"I guess this is it." Justin said sadly.

"Yes. But I'll see you again in the spring. We *all* will."

"Take good care of Andraleena for me."

"You can count on it."

With nothing more to be said, Pitter turned to go, then stopped.

"Hey, Justin," he called to the small boy walking away.

"What?" Justin asked.

"I cherish the day, I found the Land of Faye! That rhymes. I *love* rhymes. Did I tell you that?"

"Yes! A hundred times!"

Some Plants Mentioned

Below is a listing of some of the plants mentioned in **Beyond Betwixt Between**. Those that are native to the United States are indicated with an 'N' following the name. Both the common name and Latin binomial are given to aid identification.

American Ginseng (*Panax quinquefolius*) N
Black Cohosh (*Cimicifuga racemosa*) N
Black-eyed Susan (*Rudbeckia hirta*) N
Bloodroot (*Sanguinaria canadensis*) N
Blue Vervain (*Verbena hastata*) N
Butterflyweed (*Asclepias tuberosa*) N
Cardinal Flower (*Lobelia cardinalis*) N
Chicory (*Cichorium intybus*)
Common Milkweed (*Asclepias syriaca*) N
Evening Primrose (*Oenothera biennis*) N
Forget-Me-Not (*Myosotis verna*) N
Goldenrod (*Solidago odora*) N
Goldenseal (*Hydrastis canadensis*) N
Horsetail (*Equisetum arvense*) N
Hyssop (*Hyssopus officinalis*)
Indian Pipe - Fairy Smoke (*Monotropa uniflora*) N
Jewelweed (*Impatiens capensis*) N
Lady's-slipper (*Cypripedium calceolus*) N
Lamb's Ears (*Stachys byzantina*)
Lavender (*Lavandula angustifolia*)
Lemongrass (*Cymbopogon citratus*)
Lovage (*Levisticum officinale*)
Marshmallow (*Althaea officinalis*)
Mayapple (*Podophyllum pelatum*) N
Purple Coneflower (*Echinacea purpurea*) N
Queen Anne's Lace (*Daucus carota*)
Rose Geranium (*Pelargonium graveolens*)
Rosemary (*Rosmarinus officinalis*)
Skunk Cabbage (*Symplocarpus foetidus*) N
Soapwort - Bouncing Bet (*Saponaria officinalis*)
Sweetgrass (*Hierochloe odorata*) N
Thyme (*Thymus vulgaris / sp.*)
Trout Lily (*Erythronium americanum*) N
Violet (*Viola cucullata, Viola pedata*) N
Wild Bergamot (*Monarda fistulosa*) N
Wild Ginger (*Asarum canadense*) N

Getting Involved

Regardless of what you may or may not believe about the existence of nature spirits and fairies, the threat to native plants is real. Although it is already too late for some, there is hope for those that are still struggling to survive against incredible odds. An increased awareness and call to action is sweeping the country, spearheaded by dedicated groups and individuals with vision. I encourage you to get involved in teaching children about nature and the plant kingdom, and in planting and protecting our native botanical heritage, either on your own or through groups like the ones listed here.

United Plant Savers
P O Box 98
East Barre, VT 05649

A non-profit organization founded by renowned herbalist and educator, Rosemary Gladstar. UpS is dedicated to saving endangered and threatened medicinal plants with a focus on native American species. Promotes awareness, education, ethical wildcrafting, replanting, and the preservation of diversity. Benefits include a bi-annual newsletter, a directory of sources for cultivated plants, eligibility for grants, planting stock, etc. Sponsors educational conferences and has established a botanical reserve in southeastern Ohio. UpS is a national organization that encourages the formation of local chapters. Individual membership: $35.00

Wild Ones
P O Box 23576
Milwaukee WI 53223-0576

A non-profit organization dedicated to promoting biodiversity, environmentally sound growing practices and the appreciation and use of native plants in developing gardens, lawns and other landscapes. Wild Ones focuses on educating members and sharing information with them and the public at large. Membership includes an informative bimonthly journal and a handbook packed with helpful information. Wild Ones is a national organization with local chapters in nine states and growing. Individual membership: $20.00

Many states and localities also have native plant societies. You can often find information regarding such groups at libraries, through your local newspaper, or other garden organizations.

Turning Vision Into Reality

Across the land, groups and individuals are rallying to save our threatened and endangered native plants. Replanting projects of all shapes and sizes are in the works. While all are vital and enormously commendable, few will probably capture national attention like the one being developed by Museums At Prophetstown outside Lafayette, Indiana. This visionary endeavor encompasses land that was once the site of the historic Prophetstown Village founded by the Shawnee Chief, Tecumseh and his brother, the Prophet. It was here that the course of history for Native Americans, native plants and landscape, and European settlers, was changed forever by the Battle of Tippecanoe in 1811.

Museums At Prophetstown, (a non-profit corporation), is a monumental undertaking that involves three different museums: A 65,000 sq. ft. Woodland Native American Center, a 1920's era Wabash Valley Living History Farm, and a Prairie Environmental Center. Each of these museums will focus much of their attention on native plants.

The Wabash Valley Living History Farm will include gardens and crop lands indicative of the 1920 time period. Visitors will be able to tour a 1918 Sears Roebuck farmhouse and outbuildings, and see herbs and vegetables growing in the gardens. Costumed interpreters will recreate daily life on the farm and offer visitors a chance to get hands-on experience.

The Woodland Native American Center will be a mecca for educational exhibits and programs on Native American heritage. The story of their development of corn (maize) will be featured, not only in indoor exhibits, but in an actual Native American garden that will also include the other members of a "Three Sisters Garden", beans and squash. Visitors to these gardens will learn about the plants and the gardening practices used by Native Americans.

And last, but by no means least, will be the Prairie Environmental Center which will provide the backdrop for everything else. Over 200 acres of native prairie grasses, wildflowers, and herbs will be replanted. An old remnant woodland will be left intact, while other woodland areas and wetlands will be restored with native plants, trees, shrubs and grasses. When the major portion of the work is done, visitors will be able to hike woodland and prairie trails and see a rich diversity of native plants almost unheard of today. The Museums At Prophetstown campus will provide a much needed sanctuary for threatened and endangered native plants and create a learning laboratory of major significance.

The scope of Museums At Prophetstown goes far beyond the local community or even the state of Indiana. When completed, it will impact the preservation of heritage and native plants on a national and, perhaps even international level. I urge everyone to get involved in being a part of its realization. What we do now is our gift and our legacy to those who follow. As MAP's slogan aptly states, "From the hearts of this generation, to the hands of the next - we must pass on our heritage." Native plants are at the core of it all.

**For information, membership, volunteer
opportunities, contributions, etc., contact:**
Museums At Prophetstown
22 N Second Street   Lafayette, IN 47901   765-423-4617

Suggested Reading

Below is a listing of books that are sure to enhance your knowledge and enjoyment of herbs, native plants, wildflowers, nature, and the world of folklore. This is only a tiny sampling of the thousands of books available on these subjects. Your local library or book seller should be able to assist you with finding these publications or send a self-addressed, stamped envelope to the publishers of this book for source information.

Hedgemaids And Fairy Candles - The Lives and Lore of North American Wildflowers by Jack Sanders

Magic and Medicine of Plants by Contributing Editors and Writers of Reader's Digest.

The Complete Book of Herbs by Lesley Bremness

Wild Roots - A Forager's Guide to the Edible and Medicinal Roots, Tubers, Corms, and Rhizomes of North America by Doug Elliott

The Best of Thymes and *Christmas Thyme At Oak Hill Farm* by Marge Clark

Mrs. Reppert's TwelveMonth Herbal and others by Bertha Reppert

Are There Faeries At The Bottom Of Your Garden and others by Betsy Williams

Mugworts in May by Linda Ours Rago

Enchantment of the Faerie Realm by Ted Andrews

Cunningham's Encyclopedia of Magical Herbs by Scott Cunningham

Garden Spells - An Enchanting Collection of Victorian Wisdom by Claire Nahmad

Magic Gardens - A Modern Chronicle of Herbs and Savory Seeds by Rosetta E. Clarkson

Thyme of Death and *Loves Lies Bleeding* as well as others in the China Bayles herbal mystery series by Susan Wittig Albert

The Healing Earth - Nature's Medicine For The Troubled Soul by Philip Sutton Chard

The Native Plant Primer by Carole Ottesen

The Herb Companion a glossy, full-color bimonthly magazine devoted to growing and using herbs. PO Box 55295, Boulder CO 80322-5295

Sources For Propagated Native Plants

Those concerned with the destruction of habitat and the plight of native species, strongly oppose the gathering of plant stocks from wild sources. While it was once difficult to find propagated native wildflowers, herbs and grasses through nurseries, this is no longer the case. Many concerned small businesses now offer a large selection of native plants that have not been collected in the wild, but grown in their nurseries. Below is a listing of just a few of these sources.

Enchanter's Garden
HC77 Box 108
Hinton, WV 25951
Mail order catalog offers a large selection
of native plants, including those mentioned in this book.

Sylvan Botanicals
P O Box 91
Cooperstown, NY 13326
Specializes in American ginseng and goldenseal. Propagated rootlets and plants of various sizes. They are said to be the largest supplier of ginseng planting stock in the Northeast.

Wild Earth Native Plant Nursery
P O Box 7258
Freehold NJ 07728
Their catalog ($2.00) offers a number of the native plants included in this book, plus ferns, shrubs and vines.

Great Basin Natives
P O Box 114
Holden UT 84636
Their mail order plant list does not include plants featured in this book, but offers native plants that are indigenous to the western states.

Legendary Ethnobotanical Resources
16245 SW 304 Street
Leisure City FL 33033
Extensive catalog of native plants and seeds and many interesting gardening and herbal items.

Prairie Nursery
P O Box 306
Westfield WI 53964
A full-color catalog and growing guide featuring a large selection of native prairie wildflowers and grasses.

About The Author

Carla J. Nelson is the author and editor/publisher of **Herb Gatherings,** "The Newsletter For The Thymes", a national, bimonthly mini-magazine in its sixth year of publication, and author of the **No Thyme To Cook Herbal Gourmet** cookbook. She is a member of United Plant Savers, the Herb Society of America, the Garden Writers Association of America, the Herb Society of Central Indiana, the Herb Growing & Marketing Network, and Museums At Prophetstown. She has founded two herb organizations, organized herb events and gives classes and workshops on a wide variety of herbal topics. She and her husband, Rich, live in rural Lafayette, Indiana.

For ordering information or to schedule a program or book signing contact the publisher at the address below. To subscribe to **Herb Gatherings** "The Newsletter For The Thymes" (a twenty-page eclectic mix of herb, garden and nature related information),send $15.00 for six issues to the address below.

Herb Gatherings, Incorporated
10949 East 200 South
Lafayette, IN 47905-9453

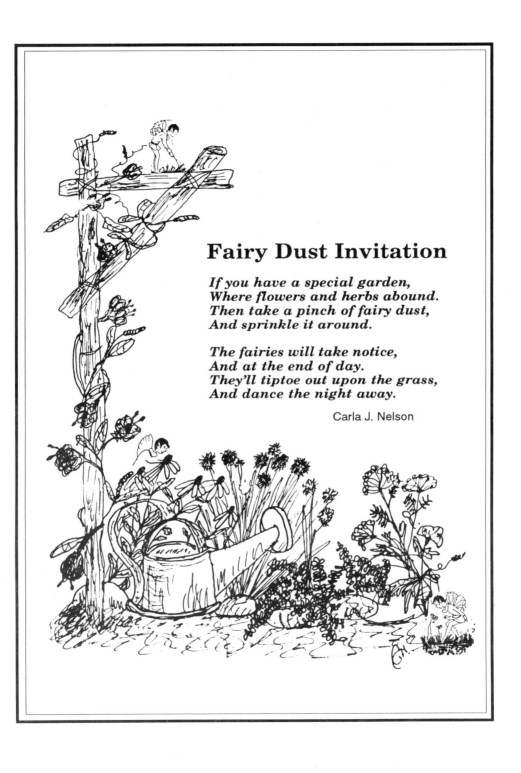

Fairy Dust Invitation

If you have a special garden,
Where flowers and herbs abound.
Then take a pinch of fairy dust,
And sprinkle it around.

The fairies will take notice,
And at the end of day.
They'll tiptoe out upon the grass,
And dance the night away.

Carla J. Nelson